Blind Spot

By Randy Russell

BLIND SPOT
HOT WIRE

Blind Spot
A Rooster Franklin Mystery

RANDY RUSSELL

A CRIME CLUB BOOK
Doubleday
NEW YORK   LONDON   TORONTO   SYDNEY   AUCKLAND

A Crime Club Book
PUBLISHED BY DOUBLEDAY

a division of Bantam Doubleday Dell Publishing Group, Inc.
666 Fifth Avenue, New York, New York 10103

DOUBLEDAY and the portrayal of a man
with a gun are trademarks of Doubleday,
a division of Bantam Doubleday Dell
Publishing Group, Inc.

Library of Congress Cataloging-in-Publication Data

Russell, Randy.
    Blind spot: a Rooster Franklin mystery / Randy Russell.—1st
ed.
    p. cm.
    I. Title.
PS3568.U7695B57   1990
813'.54—dc20   90-30190
                                                             CIP

ISBN 0-385-41563-X

M

Blind Spot

Prologue

Downtown Kansas City is as off-Broadway as off-Broadway gets. It wasn't so much the quality of the production as the quality of the audience that drove home this point to Forrest Jennings. At six-three, he stood out in his tuxedo during intermission. It was opening night and few others were in formal wear.

The lobby of the Folly Theater was crowded with smokers. There'd been more or less a classless scramble for the rest rooms. Perhaps those attending the play would have been happier had they been served buttered popcorn. Forrest, eyeing Harold Muleford suspiciously, held a slim gold lighter to the bowl of his pipe and puffed until the carefully tamped, fragrant tobacco ignited.

Forrest had made up his mind not to acknowledge Muleford's bulldog presence. There was no point. Harold shouldn't have been there to begin with. What Harold appreciated in theater lay somewhere between a painted mouth on the thumb and forefinger of a bad comic and the practiced agility of a stripper able to pick up a rolled dollar bill without using her hands.

Art was too good for this cow town, Forrest rued. It was bad enough that Muleford wore a plaid sports jacket to the opening of *Anthony Rises*. The uncouth Harold Muleford to his own and the city's blatant discredit sported a cheap, plastic camera hung around his fat neck on a strap.

Forrest had watched from his seat in near horror as the ushers time and again were forced to warn Kansas City's "King of Trucking" against using his camera during the performance. The actors had been stunned repeatedly by its automatic flash.

Harold Muleford ignored them.

As if he needed a flash in the first place, Forrest thought, drawing in his cheeks with acidic distaste. The glare of the houselights from his bald pate should have provided ample illumination for the taking of photographs. Forrest thought to ask him if he had his hair done in the wax-lane of one of the numerous car washes Harold owned in Kansas City.

Anthony Rises wasn't that good, but it was an original play. That was important to Forrest, and it should have been important to Kansas City. The play had been written by a graduate drama student at the University of Missouri, who had directly benefited by one of the dozens of scholarships Forrest sponsored in the humanities programs at the school. The cast party, in fact, would be held at the Jennings home on Ward Parkway. Harold, most definitely, was not invited. The mayor and two state legislators, however, were.

Forrest was roughly jostled by a stranger on his left, nearly knocking his pipe from his hand. The tall man turned disdainfully as he was suddenly bumped on his right. The two men then grabbed both of his arms and Forrest wondered if he'd ever seen them before as his pipe bounced on the lobby carpet, spilling embers. Someone he couldn't see at all was behind him, grasping his waist, nearly lifting him from the floor. Forrest Jennings struggled briefly, looking more shocked than threatened.

People in the crowd gasped as a uniformed security guard stepped between them and Forrest's assailants. A fourth man appeared directly in front of him, his features drawn with determination, and Forrest gave up the fight. He'd been had, he realized, and he damn well knew who was behind this plebeian assault. Nothing Muleford could do or could cause to have done to Forrest would get him even. No prank the fat man could pull would equal Forrest's recent *coup de grace* against Harold Muleford.

The assault was a futile gesture. Harold had been defeated by Jennings' own hand. What they wanted didn't matter. His ruby cuff links? His watch? Maybe they were going to pin a *Hopping to Please: Jack Rabbit Transit* button on his lapel.

The man in front of him pushed up Forrest's cummerbund and tore at his suspender clasps. The man then opened Forrest's fly and jerked down his trousers and undershorts.

The crowd in the lobby gasped. Forrest crimsoned. It was just like Harold Muleford to have Jennings "depantsed" in public.

"Hold him up," the man demanded as Forrest was pushed backward into the cradling arms of the man behind him. The crowd moved closer. Someone was laughing. "Oh look!" It was a woman's voice. The fourth man was vigorously shaking a small aerosol can. The red enamel paint was cold as it coated Forrest's groin area with an intolerable stickiness.

Forrest Jennings trembled with anger. The security guard was doing nothing to help. The man with the spray-paint disappeared and Forrest was released, swinging his arms ineffectively. Harold Muleford stepped quickly forward, flashing his dime-store camera. Forrest straightened, stepped forward and fell as his tangled slacks caught his ankles. The stupid son of a bitch was standing over him, grinning like a cat, snapping more photographs.

Forrest found he had to stand up to pull up his pants. He'd never been angrier; but he wasn't embarrassed. To be embarrassed would mean Harold Muleford's little prank had worked. It hadn't. Forrest was left suddenly alone, reaching for his pipe.

"No problem, no problem," he muttered abstractedly,

noticing that some of the crimson paint had spotted the carpet.

The security guard finally moved to help him. Another man in uniform appeared at his side, offering assistance. Forrest maintained his dignity through it all, but a renewed hatred burned in him, a hatred so intense he thought he might be consumed from the inside out. Defeating Muleford hadn't been enough. For the moment at least, Forrest Jennings thought quite seriously of having the fat man killed.

"Are you all right?" a young woman asked, stepping around the guards. "Mr. Jennings, are you all right?" She was an usher.

His left arm was bruised, but it was nothing. Forrest tried to laugh.

"It's part of the play, really," he insisted, then repeated himself more loudly so that he might be overheard by some of the still-gaping rubberneckers. The young lady's look of utter concern was disarming.

It wouldn't be in the papers. Forrest would see to that. Others now were trying to help. And he would see to it that the security guards who had assisted in Harold's dainty drama were summarily dismissed. Perhaps she was a student, he thought.

The thick coating of red paint hardened his shirttails.

"Would you care to see me home?" he said to her as he zipped up. "I'm afraid I may need a little assistance with . . . with *this.*" She nodded bravely, a nurse tending the fallen soldier. Forrest liked that.

Partially it was his own fault, he knew, for having appeared in public without a bodyguard. But mostly, Forrest Jennings was determined to make that bastard pay for this, too.

CHAPTER ONE

Stealing a car was the last thing on Alton Franklin's mind as he stepped from the noisy crowd of sixty thousand to the $100 window on the upper level of the south grand-stand at Oaklawn Park, in Hot Springs, Arkansas, to play a hunch. With the clear, even voice of a man conducting serious business, he placed $2,000 to win on the seven horse, You'll Be Surprised, a three-year-old filly with an unimpressive early career. It was his entire betting pool for the day, of which a maximum bet was supposed to be no more than 25 percent.

A skinny young man in gold-rimmed glasses was watching Alton. The blond youth wore a gray-and-white striped suit over a bright green golf shirt. His polished brown wing tips looked like shoes you wore because someone else told you to.

Alton didn't like being watched—especially today. It hadn't been his year at the racetrack. In truth, it hadn't been his two and a half years at the racetrack. He'd been counting on the Oaklawn season to get him back on the winning track. It was the last day of the meet and so far the Oaklawn Jockey Club had been as unkind to Alton's expert handicapping as the previous seasons at other tracks in the South and along the East Coast had been.

Carefully folding his $2,000 ticket into his program, the thirty-two-year-old "retired" thief slipped his imme-diate future into the inside pocket of his wrinkled, blue blazer. It was his lucky jacket, the one he always wore to the races.

"The only luck at a racetrack is bad luck," an old handicapper had told him once as they huddled under the bleachers during a sudden rain at Louisiana Downs. "When you win, luck ain't involved. Cashing that ticket means you figured things out right. When something happens to keep you from winning, that's called luck— bad luck."

Alton had had about all the luck he could stand. He'd lost considerable faith in his own calculations. The horses in the fifth race had warmed up and were making their way to the starting gate. Most of the crowd was hurrying to get back to their seats.

Alton could no longer watch the bits and pieces of bad luck happen to him. The race itself was nothing more than a small slice of time you had to live through. He didn't care how the race happened, as long as it happened. You'll Be Surprised either won or she didn't. Alton wanted it over and done with.

Having some kid in brown shoes and a striped suit watch you place a bet was bad luck. Alton marched around and squeezed between the anonymous others on his way to the men's room. It had become his escape from the dramatic tension of watching a race he'd bet heavily on. His confidence, having been kicked hard, was rolled over on its side, quivering. The rest rooms, he'd learned, were virtually empty during a race.

Alton had developed a blind spot. An important factor was eluding his handicapping, a factor in the past performances, the workout reports, the ever changing track bias. Something about the jockeys, the trainers, the gate position. Something in the horse's speed, the pace of the race, the distance, the horse's class, form or fitness. Something he couldn't put his finger on.

And Alton was as convinced of its existence as he was convinced that he just couldn't see it. A blind spot.

He fought valiantly not to think of the money he'd lost as he briefly paused to check the lighted tote board, mounted high on the cinder-block wall above the betting windows, before stepping into the men's room. Alton spied the blond man, who moved confusedly as he decided which way to go. Holding his folded program in one hand, the skinny youth in wire glasses turned first one way then the other, looked down at his program then up at the tote monitor, then turned again as if the answer he sought could be found painted on the back of one of the scurrying gamblers making his way to the windows. Alton wished him luck.

The horses had reached the starting gate. All Alton wanted to know was the winning number once the race was over. Alton was prepared to lose. Hell, he knew how to lose, and if you don't leave a little blood at the track you haven't been to the races. But lately, betting on the horses felt like falling in love with a vampire. Alton was being sucked dry.

He should have put no more than $50 on You'll Be Surprised. That was his action money, the maximum Alton allowed himself each day for betting hunches. Instead, he'd put $2,000 on the chocolate-colored filly because he needed the money, the worst reason in the world for betting a hunch with a saddle and a number on her blanket.

Alton had bet a long shot to save his ass and he had to remind himself now that he was a professional handicapper, a man who shrewdly worked the edges of the percentages of win and lose as a fakir might walk the sharpened edge of a long knife.

Propped up in bed with his calculator and notebooks, Alton had spent the night in his room at the Majestic painstakingly handicapping the past performances of every horse entered in Saturday's races. In the morning, sitting in the downstairs restaurant, he went over his notes and made numerical entries in the day's program. He referred time and time again to his marked-up copy of the *Daily Racing Form*.

Satisfied that he had transferred all the information he

needed, he discarded the newspaper. Things had gotten so bad that he had taken to actually reading the articles in the *Daily Form.*

Alton had written *Skip it* across the top of the fifth-race entries in his program. He narrowed his day's work to one race, the ninth. But, after taking his seat in the grandstands, he noticed something odd about the fifth race. It looked to Alton as if somebody was trying to pull a fast one.

Dutifully, he'd penned in the jockey changes for all races. Glancing at the fifth race, Alton had felt the clouds parting and a light beginning to shine from somewhere over his shoulder. Rough Breaks was the morning-line co-favorite under Oaklawn's premiere jockey, Pat Day. But two other fillies in the fifth interested Alton.

Both horses were trained by D. Wayne Lukas but were going off as separate wagers because they had different owners. That's the way it worked in Arkansas. Special Gift, owned by Eugene V. Klein, shared low odds with Rough Breaks. It made sense. Special Gift was a lightly raced youngster out of Seattle Slew and she'd already proven she could carry speed to the final turn, which was what a handicapper looked for when judging a three-year-old in the spring of her racing career.

But the jockeys were wrong. That was the rub. Scott Stevens got the mount on Special Gift and the odds at post time had risen to seven-to-one and rightly so. The smart money had jumped to the other favorite. Rough Breaks was going off at even money by the time Alton had made his way to the window.

Scott Stevens was a new jockey with an untested track record. He was not the jockey any trainer would have chosen for a strong effort in a major allowance race. Scott's older brother, however, was as tested as a jockey came. Gary Stevens, an absolute top rider at the peak of his form, had taken the mount on Lukas' other horse,

You'll Be Surprised. She was morning-lined in the seven-horse field as the long shot at twelve-to-one.

The crowd was right to lay off Special Gift, but they'd made a mistake in jumping onto Pat Day's mount and overlooking the long shot. Lukas had moved the veteran jockey to the number-seven horse for a reason. Lukas was out to win with You'll Be Surprised. And so was Alton. Even his two thousand on her nose couldn't keep the odds short on You'll Be Surprised and she slipped to thirteen-to-one as Alton entered the rest room.

He locked the stall door as the loudspeaker in the men's room faintly announced that the seventh horse was being loaded into the gate. Alton's guts tightened. He pressed his foot on the flushing mechanism to drown out the call of the race as the bells sounded that closed the betting windows.

They were off.

With both hands over his ears, Alton came as close to praying as he ever did when playing the horses. He fought hard to make his mind a blank.

Allowing time for a possible photo finish or a disqualification, Alton kept the toilet flushing even after he heard the dim roar of the huge crowd as the horses crossed the finish line. Men began trickling into the rest room, cursing their luck. Despite his efforts not to, Alton overheard that the favored Rough Breaks hadn't won.

It was the losers who came into the rest room. The men with bragging rights were already making their way to the windows to cash tickets or were basking happily in their seats.

Alton would know the outcome once he made his way into the grandstand clubhouse to check the lighted finish board. Either the number seven would be lighted on top, or it wouldn't be. It was that simple. In his string of losses, Alton had reduced the thunderous excitement of a horse race, with all its possibilities of injury and glory, to a mere roll of the dice.

Someone bumped into him then walked away. Alton stared at the board.

He'd been right. The number seven was on top, haloed in light. D. Wayne Lukas and Gary Stevens had brought her in. He didn't care how they'd managed it, only that they had. Pat Day had kept Rough Breaks up for place and a mid-field horse had come in third. Special Gift finished out of the money.

Alton felt like shouting. His skin danced. It felt good. The money he'd won should have shaken him at least a little. But being right was all that mattered. Being right on a long shot made him suddenly King of the World. You'll Be Surprised, he told himself, hadn't surprised him at all. She'd only done exactly what he'd expected her to and paid $28.20 to $2 to win.

Of the sixty thousand gamblers at the track, he'd been the only one, he believed, who'd bet big money on the long shot to win.

"Screw you all," Alton said to himself as he made his way to a downstairs window to cash his $28,200 ticket. He filled out the required tax form at the cashier's desk, using a false identification card and a made-up Social Security number. The IRS kept 20 percent and he was still up more than $8,000 for the month. Oaklawn had saved his ass, after all. Alton only wondered why it had taken so long.

Before leaving the windows, he placed his bet for the ninth race, the Arkansas Derby. He'd been able to toss out the favorite last night, a California shipper named Mi Preferido burdened with 126 pounds for the mile-and-an-eighth route. California horses, accustomed to the lightning-fast hard surfaces of that state's tracks, rarely did well the first time around Oaklawn's loamy oval. With the extra weight, Mi Preferido was a cinch to lose.

Only Notebook and Proper Reality were standouts in the $500,000 Grade I event. Notebook's past performances indicated the colt was tiring, falling off form.

Last night it had seemed obvious to Alton that the colt needed more rest between races. That left Proper Reality, carrying 118 pounds and clearly ready to win if he could handle the field. Alton bet that he could.

Popular locally, Proper Reality was morning-lined at four-to-one and had been Alton's best bet of the day before his hunch had come along. His confidence restored, Alton ended the Oaklawn meet with $5,000 on Proper Reality to show. Even if Proper Reality stumbled twice or they gave Mi Preferido beach thongs to run in, Alton still looked to double his money as long as Proper Reality came in third.

Alton made his way to the beer and hot-dog concession to celebrate, while the plungers and jump bettors fretted over the mediocre seventh and eighth races. He chose to stand in the longest of three lines and waited his turn, trying hard not to smile.

"Hello, Princess," he called to the dark-haired girl pulling beers into plastic souvenir cups.

She smiled without looking up. Monique Rene Wolfert worked as a cocktail waitress in the Magnolia Room at the Majestic. She filled in days at the track when the crowds were especially large. During the season, she and Alton had gotten to know each other. Monique had taken to spending the night in Alton's room during the past few weeks. Now that he'd finally won, Alton Franklin looked forward to enjoying her company that night and most of Sunday morning as Hot Springs National Park emptied of the thousands of tourists come for the last weekend of racing.

He pushed five across the elevated counter and picked up his beer and hot dog.

"Keep the change," he sang nonchalantly. Under the five, he'd placed a crisp, new C-note. It was bad form not to tip after hitting a big bet.

Monique's perfectly round, dark eyes shot open as she discovered the hidden hundred.

"Dammit, Frankie," she said gleefully, "you had Gary Stevens' long shot, didn't you!"

"Let's just say that I've discovered a Proper Reality," Alton chided, knowing she'd have the runner, who carried bets to and from the windows for employees, put the C-note on his pick for the feature race.

"I just hope you won enough to buy a new jacket," she said, back to pulling beers.

Alton turned with his beer and hot dog, heading for the condiment counter, and bumped into the thin youth in the gray-and-white suit. A little beer sloshed on the skinny kid's green shirt. Wide, pale eyes blinked at Alton through the thick lenses of his glasses. The kid looked nervous.

"Sorry," Alton mumbled. The young man didn't say anything.

"The number-one horse in the ninth," Alton said, winking. He stepped around the clod's brown wing tips. "We'll call it even," Alton added just in case the youngster didn't know he was being given Alton's best bet of the day.

Alton found his assigned seat in the grandstands and thoroughly enjoyed watching the races leading up to the ninth. Horses he'd figured to come from behind did, in fact, put on powerful stretch runs. Horses he'd pegged to tire wore down at the sixteenth pole as if on Alton's command.

It was a wonderfully warm April afternoon in the South and there were pretty women everywhere in the crowd, women he hadn't had time to notice until today. Women with bright, glistening eyes and full lips. Women in wide-brimmed spring hats and women in tight shorts. Women that Alton believed you could bet on to smile back at you when you finally caught their eye. Women you could bet on to look shyly the other way.

The horses for the feature race were saddled in the infield. Alton broke a cardinal rule of the professional horseplayer by telling the people sitting around him which horse he'd put his money on in the Arkansas Derby. He talked quite a few of them into getting off the favorite. Though impressive on the West Coast, Mi Preferido hadn't had a workout since being shipped to Oaklawn. He pointed out to them that Proper Reality had two superb workouts in the last week and was clearly ready to run.

When the expensive and beautiful thoroughbreds were led one by one into the starting gate, Alton Franklin rose to his feet to cheer them on, his $5,000 ticket clutched tightly in his hand, his heart racing with the excitement of a good contest, with the thrilling possibility of being proven right in the midst of the clamorous noise of the horses and the crowd. He held the immediate future in his hand. And in his heart he held the transient belief that, while the real world surely turned, it wouldn't turn against him.

It was a quiet celebration. Alton sat at his usual table in the sedate Magnolia Room, by the windows that overlooked the swimming pool.

A couple stood in the shallow end, hugging each other in the eerie illumination of electric lights upon water at night. Spotlights hidden in the azalea bushes made the surrounding blossoms look like hideous faces on skinny sticks. A white towel lay on the diving board like a puddle that needed mopping up. Alton worried about Churchill Downs.

He'd be in Louisville in time for the races on Tuesday and he desperately needed more than one good bet if he meant to end the year in the black. There'd been a subtle shift in the emphasis in horse racing, a nuance more important than speed, that he was overlooking. Alton promised himself if he hadn't doubled his earnings by May, he'd skip the Kentucky Derby.

The Magnolia Room was tucked away inside the Majestic Hotel. The rowdy crowd was downstairs at the piano bar. The tourists who hadn't left town had made their way to one of Hot Springs' more popular night spots down the street, loud places that featured laughter and dance bands. The Magnolia Room was on its last leg. Alton and a few of the season regulars liked it this way, but the word was it wouldn't open for next year's racing meet.

There was nothing to do on Sunday, no races to worry over, and this was his one chance to get drunk. Alton sipped his glass of scotch and chased it with a swig of cool beer. Two men chatted in soft undertones at the bar. A few other tables were occupied. Nick Nadri, the resident one-man band, had the drum machine turned down low and played forgettable numbers on the keyboard.

If Alton got too drunk and chucked his shot glass across the room, people here would understand. Damn, he wanted to bet that race again. He wanted a long shot to play tomorrow and the next day and the day after that. He had no way of knowing if the long shot would be there again. There was a lifetime of nagging failures both large and small to convince him that even if the horse did run again he would miss the bet next time.

Alton watched Monique, in her cocktail miniskirt and fishnet hose, take a drink order from a young couple who looked sorely out of place. The girl smiled nervously as if she were being watched. The fellow with her kept looking around to see if he was missing something. There was nothing to miss. People came to the Magnolia Room for what wasn't there, not for what was.

It might not be the couple's first visit to the racetrack, but it was their first time in the Majestic's second-floor club. The bet was whether or not they finished their drinks before leaving.

Monique was genetically bubbly, and Alton liked watching her work. You'd have thought the place was packed by the way she bounced between tables, smiling from side to side, back to the bar with her empty tray. There was a gleam about Monique and she was going with him to Louisville, where she had work lined up for the Churchill season. They'd stay together for a little while, Alton figured, at least until she ran across a gambler with a flashier style, someone nearer her age and a bit livelier.

A shadow crossed his table. Alton glanced up to see the kid in the gray-and-white striped suit standing over him. He had changed into a shirt and tie and was holding two bottled beers, peering questioningly at the gambler.

"I wanted to thank you for that tip," he said, his voice cracking. The skinny kid wasn't good at meeting people. Alton nodded and the youth held out to him a beer.

"Mind if I join you?"

"Help yourself," Alton said, wary as he watched him pull out a chair from the small, round table. He cleared his throat and started talking before he'd fully sat down.

"I'm James Spivey from Kansas City."

Alton didn't offer to shake hands. Instead, he leaned back in his chair and finished off his original beer, sat the bottle down and switched Spivey's bottle of beer to his right hand.

"I hope you don't mind if I ask, but you're a professional horseplayer, aren't you? I mean, you guys really do exist? You make your living like this?"

"Cut the crap," Alton barked, not believing Spivey's line. "Gambling's a solitary life. It's hotels and whores. In case nobody's ever told you, you tend to get their names mixed up."

"A suitcase and a gun?" Spivey asked, changing tones. "I'm an attorney, Mr. Franklin," he said, squinting behind his thick wire-rim glasses.

"I'm not here to meet new people," Alton said. He thought of a hundred good reasons he didn't want a Kansas City lawyer asking him questions.

"I guess not," Spivey said. "The girl at the hot-dog stand told me your name." He tilted his head clandestinely toward the bar where Monique stood, beaming her silly good mood across the dimly lit room. Spivey fingered the bottle of beer on the table, did not drink it.

"Well, it was awfully damn nice to meet you," Alton said, attempting to finalize their conversation. "I hope you don't think I'm being rude, but I'm expecting friends."

Alton gestured with his left hand, inviting Spivey to take his leave anytime he felt like it, preferably soon. Alton recalled the way the kid with the ugly shoes had been watching him at the $100 window. It was obviously no mistake he'd fallen in line behind Alton at the concession stand following the fifth race. It was even less of a coincidence that the boy lawyer had found him here.

"I guess I didn't drop by just to say hi," Spivey sputtered. "I—"

"I guess I really don't give a sock full of shit," Alton cut him off. He turned to look out the window at the crazy flower-faces decorating the shrubbery around the pool.

"But you should, Mr. Franklin . . ."

"You've been asked to leave," Alton said clearly, still not looking at him.

"Ray Sargent sent me," the kid said. "I work for him, and we've got a job for you."

CHAPTER TWO

Alton Franklin twisted his head sideways and stared at the blinking eyes behind the youth's glasses, finding there a steely intensity that belied the lawyer's age. Something big was up. Alton believed he wanted no part of it.

Ray Sargent was the head of Sargent Security, a concrete-and-glass corporation now headquartered in Kansas City, with branch offices in several major cities across the country. Alton couldn't imagine why the old ex-cop would go to this much trouble to be bothering him now. Their shared history was something they both wanted to forget, a bank robbery gone bad.

It had been Alton's first heist of anything worth more than a new Camaro on the black market. A petty car thief then, Alton was relentlessly hounded by the security expert, who had worked for the bank as a consultant at the time. It had ended with people dead and with an uneasy truce between Alton and Ray Sargent. But it had ended.

The bank's money officially never turned up, though Alton and Ray Sargent each knew what they'd done with every penny of their halves. Alton had left Kansas City for good and it only made proper sense that he and Ray Sargent should never see each other again.

Ray Sargent knew Alton Franklin as a car thief. But if he wanted a car stolen, there were plenty of high school kids who could do that for him.

"It's rather sensitive," Spivey went on, thinking he'd

piqued Alton's curiosity. "Ray said you could be trusted, Rooster."

That was enough. "What he meant was I could be blackmailed," Alton spat, leaning sharply forward. "You tell that son of a bitch I'm not interested."

"Nothing like that," Spivey stammered.

But Alton wasn't finished. "And nobody calls me Rooster," he seethed. "Nobody." Words weren't needed to express the threat in Alton's brown eyes.

Spivey nodded solemnly. "Nothing like blackmail," he finally said, weakly. "Nothing like that at all. I, uh, I brought the money with me. Ray said you'd want it in cash."

"What else did he say?" Alton leaned back, his hand tightening on the beer bottle.

"He said you owed him a favor and he figured you needed the work." Spivey's voice cracked. He swallowed. "A hundred thousand. Half 'n' half. I can bring it to your room."

He paused, waiting to be asked what the job was.

Alton stared at a spot in the middle of the kid's forehead, thinking to put his beer bottle there.

"It's clean money, Mr. Franklin, if that's what you're worried about."

"Double it," Alton said. "Double it and I have to talk to Ray." Doubling an offer was the acid test. If they were willing to even consider paying him $200,000, Alton would know he was being set up.

"I'm afraid that's impossible," Spivey said, sounding more and more like an attorney.

"Which?"

"Both probably, but talking to Ray is what I meant. He's out of the country."

"And you're out of time," Alton said. "There are people here who will help you leave." Alton glanced across the room to see if the bartender was watching them. He saw Monique instead, a questioning smile wallpapering her face. He shook his head and glanced away. Alton didn't need her bouncing over to say something cheerful.

"Give me a minute?" Spivey asked. "Ray Sargent's out of the country. If it's absolutely necessary, it might be possible to get a call back to you. But you haven't heard what the job is yet. It's fairly simple, actually."

Alton waited.

"We want you to place a bid for us at an auction."

"That's it? I don't believe it, kid. Why don't you just take the money and bid for yourself?"

"Well, it's not that simple," Spivey corrected himself. "We need someone unknown and someone, as I said, we can trust. The item for auction is, well, unregistered, so to speak."

"Stolen." Realizing his own bottle of beer was empty, Alton released it and reached for Spivey's untouched bottle.

"Let's just say it's an illegal auction. We're dealing with the black market here, but at an extremely high level. The item we're discussing is valued in the millions."

"And who wants this car?" Alton asked, jumping to his own conclusion.

"We do, Mr. Franklin. And, yes, it is an automobile. A very special automobile. It was stolen a couple months ago and is about to be put back on the market. Now, our client is willing to pay the going price, but the seller can't know it's his bid."

"I don't work for ghosts, Mr. Attorney. Who's the client?"

"I have no say in this. I don't myself know who the client is and I can pretty much guarantee that our proposition is based in large part on the stipulation that you will serve as our proxy without knowing who the buyer is."

Alton was thinking that part over. He hated lawyers. Spivey waited until Alton had drunk from the bottle of beer and had brought it back down to the table before continuing.

"Surely, you can respect client confidentiality in matters such as these."

"And if my bid's unsuccessful?" Alton asked, switching tracks.

Spivey's eye twitched. "That's where the second half of the payment comes in, Mr. Franklin. We want that car under any circumstances and it seems you possess particular skills that would come in handy in such an eventuality."

"If I have to steal it, we're back to numbers. A car worth millions is certainly worth a couple hundred grand if this guy's bid is too low. I get a hundred thousand up front and a hundred thousand if I have to so much as start the car by myself."

"Upon delivery," Spivey said. "That's it, then. I'll see if I can authorize the new amount. If so, should I bring the initial payment and the auction packet to your room?"

"As soon as I get that phone call. You have my room number?"

"Of course," Spivey said. "But it's not that easy. There's a time difference for one thing. And Madagascar's not an easy place to call."

If $100,000 could rescue Alton's career as a horseplayer, $200,000 could see him through another long losing streak. He was also curious to see a car worth this much money, piracy and bother.

"When is this auction anyway?"

"Tuesday," Spivey answered.

"Then I damn well better get that call tonight. I'll be in my room in about an hour. Let's not keep me up too late."

Alton rose from his chair and killed the remainder of the beer. The young lawyer stood and looked puzzled for a moment. Perhaps he wanted to shake hands. It wasn't until the kid in the gray-and-white suit was walking toward the door that Alton slowly lowered the bottle from his face.

"What did that guy want?" Monique asked, sensing a conspiracy. She pushed Spivey's empty chair back up to the table, then picked up the beer bottles and placed them on her tray. She handed Alton a fresh tumbler of Johnnie Walker Red on the rocks.

"You," Alton said, teasing. He sipped his drink. "He offered me some money if I'd set you two up."

"No, really," Monique pouted.

"He wanted to thank me. I gave him Proper Reality in the feature today."

"I thought I saw him somewhere," she mused. "That was a good bet, Frankie. I made over three hundred dollars."

No doubt about that, Alton thought. Winning $8.40 against $2 on a horse that should have been the odds-on favorite was good money. He'd cleared a sizable profit himself on Proper Reality. But it was the future that concerned Alton. Buried inside of him was the numbing doubt that the long shot had been pure coincidence and he would continue picking the wrong horses for another year. Proper or improper, it was reality he struggled with as he considered taking $200,000 for something as routine as stealing a car.

And he might not even have to do that. His bid, for all he knew, would be accepted. In which case, Alton stood to clear $100,000 for not stealing a car. Now that was the kind of work a man fighting against a losing streak would like to get more of.

It was a little after 2 A.M. when the phone rang in Alton's room. Monique rolled over in her sleep as Alton pulled himself up against the headboard to answer the call. There was no mistaking Ray Sargent's gravelly baritone.

He should have been a professional wrestler. He had the voice for it.

"Who am I bidding for?" Alton asked, having given up trying to figure out what time it was in Madagascar. Sargent, it turned out, had been hired by the ambassador as a personal security consultant. Ray, Alton figured, was getting a kick out of harassing the CIA boys and the Marine guards at the embassy.

"We wouldn't want you to get into any trouble, Rooster," Ray Sargent stalled, chuckling. "Let's just say you're doing me a little favor."

Very few people still referred to Alton by his prison nickname. Ray was one of them. Alton had picked up the moniker from a multicolored tattoo of a fighting cock on his chest. The fading tattoo was a relic of a past life, a life of petty crime that had culminated in the killing of two men. They'd deserved it, but that didn't let Alton off the hook. Ray Sargent knew the details and knew as well as Alton did there was no statute of limitations for murder.

"As long as you don't start thinking I'm on the payroll," Alton warned.

Ray Sargent laughed again. "Cash works both ways. You don't have to worry about self-employment withholdings and I don't have to admit ever having heard of you if something, God forbid, should go wrong."

"It's two hundred grand then," Alton said to clarify. "If I have to *drive* it to you?"

"That's the deal. But listen, don't go getting any fancy ideas. The car is hotter than a missing Rembrandt. There are people gathering in Kansas City right now ready to kill to get their hands on it. They're preparing their own bids, if you know what I mean?"

"I don't plan on driving it across the state."

"I know that, son. That's the reason I wanted you for this one." Ray Sargent paused and Alton wondered if he was going to threaten him against a double cross.

"We've got a nice cozy place for it when the time

comes," the gravelly voice reassured him from across the ocean. "Spivey will fill you in on the logistics."

"What the hell is it anyway? Hitler's Dusenberg?"

"Don't make me laugh, Rooster. Bad ticker, you know." Ray Sargent was off the line, leaving Alton in the dark. Monique mumbled unintelligible syllables in her dreams. Alton could have used the company, but he decided to let her sleep. Sometimes women dreamed the names of winning horses. Sometimes they just dreamed.

Like someone mired in a marriage forgetting to notice his wife, Alton had missed the coming of spring. There were no horses he'd be betting on for a few days and he marveled at the resplendence of the lush green valleys as he drove north through the Ouachita Mountains of Arkansas. There were bright greens and dark greens, green softly overlapping other green. He'd never realized how many shades of green there were.

Dollar bills, too, were green. Alton tried to find a tree so large that it sprouted two hundred thousand separate green leaves. He had no idea how big a tree that would be.

"Someone should be awarded a government grant to count the number of leaves on a given tree," he said. Monique didn't reply.

From the driver's seat of his converted van, Alton pointed out a cluster of blossoming dogwood illuminated in the dappled sunlight that filtered through the taller trees. For weeks, Alton had made daily note of the precise temperature at race time, the wind direction and velocity, the humidity and the chances of precipitation. He'd studied the weather in detail as it even slightly might affect the performance of a thoroughbred and a jockey, the deepness of the track. But Alton had altogether missed the bigger picture, the change of seasons.

"What's Kansas City known for?" Monique asked again, strapped snugly in her seat belt and shoulder harness as they rode the sharp turns of the mountain highway, the road rising and falling as if taking a breath.

"Barbecue and jazz," Alton said. "And they won the World Series a few years back."

"That's it?" she asked pleasantly, trying to get him to talk. Monique turned sideways to look at him.

"Trees and wide boulevards. And lots of places to shop. Fountains."

"No racetrack?"

Alton shook his head.

"Then what are we going to Kansas City for?" she asked. She wanted a few details about what they were up to, about what had changed his plans.

"For a while," Alton answered, unable to avoid the obvious response.

"I have to see a couple people," he explained. "And do a little banking."

"I'll bet you do at that," Monique sighed. "Don't you ever lose?"

Alton had managed to keep up a facade of winning at the track through it all. That had been necessary. A gambler kept his bets to himself when he was losing. To do otherwise would risk despair. Desperation made for awkward bets and almost guaranteed failure. Handicapping horses was an objective skill and it never mattered how badly you *wanted* to win. Alton worried the same might be true of life.

"Now, now," Alton said. "Let's keep a proper reality."

"If you say that one more time, Frankie, I'll scream."

Alton laughed at himself. The horse's name had become a catch phrase for him. "All I meant was I'm not what you'd call rich." He threw on the brakes for a sharp switchback marked twenty miles-per-hour.

"You're exactly what I'd call rich," Monique countered, taking her turn to be cute. "You don't work for anybody. You live in nice hotels and eat every meal out. And you bet thousands of dollars on the horses every week."

"It's all percentages," Alton insisted. "My winnings are a certain percent of my wagers a certain percent of the time. The least little slip in the percentages and I don't cover my expenses."

"Save it for the IRS, Frankie. You got money and you know what to do to keep getting money. Hell, half the time I don't even know if the horse I bet on is going to come out of the gate frontways."

Nobody knows, Alton thought. But he didn't say anything. He'd let her think he was some kind of an American hero, if she wanted to. She'd learn soon enough. Besides, he liked her smile and there was something almost perfect about the way Monique's full breasts bounced ever so slightly when the van bottomed out off a steep hill. There was something uplifting about seeing the way they did that.

CHAPTER THREE

James Spivey pulled over to the sidewalk where it was illegal to park on Fifty-fifth Street, a few car lengths short of the stop sign at Ward Parkway. It was the heart of Kansas City's wealthiest neighborhood.

"There it is," the blond kid with a law degree told Alton, who was studying the sheer size of the massive Jennings house and lawn. The unfenced estate took up half the block and there were no trees on the property, as if the lawn were designed to have you look only at the house that curiously appeared to be always in the distance. Alton felt like a dog behind a window drooling at the outdoors.

The three-story mansion was uninviting, reminding Alton of a Carnegie library or a museum. There were the usual pillars and stone lintels, a stone and tile roof that appeared entirely too heavy to be held up by anything short of a federal courthouse.

"Looks like a fort," Spivey offered, leaning over a bit in his three-piece suit to see better out Alton's rolled-down window. A driveway led up from the street and straight back to a matching carriage house that had been outfitted with garage doors somewhere along the line.

"More like a mausoleum," Alton said. "Does anybody *live* there?"

"That's the rumor. At least when he's not in Europe."

"Great place for an auction," Alton muttered. He scrutinized the garage doors of the carriage house. The lay of the home was imposing, distanced from the street but in plain and mammoth view. It was an arrogant estate and Alton didn't like it.

"We could take it now, if you want," he told the young attorney. A good kick would get the garage doors open. Alton could have it hot-wired and on the street before anyone could hike from the house to the garage to see what was going on. He could have the damn thing across the state line and into Kansas before the police dispatched a car to answer the alarm, if there was an alarm.

Fifty percent of a successful theft was knowing what you were doing. The other half was just doing it.

"Don't be so sure," Spivey advised. "I'm afraid you're jumping to conclusions. The car's not in the garage. Not the car we want."

Alton waited to be filled in.

Spivey put the gray sedan into reverse and eased backward along Fifty-fifth Street in the direction of State Line Road. Soon the west side of the mansion was visible.

"Notice anything about the house?" the attorney asked.

"One of the fireplace chimneys has been added."

"Recently replaced," Spivey corrected him. "Jennings had the ground floor of the back half of the house torn out, brick by brick."

"Then rebuilt." Alton smiled. "The damn thing's inside the house."

"Not that I've seen it, mind you."

"But it's in there, right? He had the wall, fireplace and all, torn down and put back up so he could drive the car right into the living room or library. What a play."

"Guess he knew you were coming, Mr. Franklin. And, take my word for it, there are no French windows or sliding-glass doors the car can be driven out through."

Alton considered Jennings' cleverness as Spivey drove them toward downtown on Southwest Trafficway. He'd heard of people who had vintage cars dismantled and rebuilt inside of buildings. This was the first time he'd heard of anyone tearing down an exterior wall and having it reerected so he could park his motorized plaything in the living room. Or bedroom, for that matter.

If he had to steal it, Alton realized, he'd be earning his money.

"Fill me in on Jennings. Family money?"

"Not really." Spivey braked for the light at Westport Road. The large face of a Metro bus idled two inches from their rear bumper. Spivey ignored it. "His father owned a jewelry store downtown, so there was a little money all along."

"Jennings Jewelry," Alton said. "Of course. The kid comes along and franchises it."

"That's him," Spivey admitted drolly. "One of the first successful franchises of its kind. High markup on diamonds, you know. And there's a Jennings Jewelry in every other shopping mall between here and L.A."

The light changed.

"Not just jewelry, Mr. Franklin. Next it was the gourmet ice cream. He hired out the lab work and came up with a hard ice cream that tastes like it was made from buttermilk, calls it *Au Natural*. Catches on like wildfire, as I'm sure you know. Of course, it's all chemically flavored."

"And it's only sold through Au Natural ice cream parlors," Alton chimed in. "And there's one of those in every other mall between here and L.A."

"Seems more like *every* mall anymore, doesn't it?" Spivey stayed carefully within the posted speed limit as vehicles on either side of the three-lane sped by him. They turned left on Thirty-first Street, just short of the WDAF-TV station, sprouting satellite dishes like mushrooms in the backyard. Thirty-first was an access road at this point, dropping narrowly down a steep hill into the industrial bottoms.

"He's into art," Spivey said in the middle of their

bumpy descent. "Make that The Arts. Symphony backer and local theater. Cultural stuff."

"And he collects cars," Alton added.

"Not at all. But this car is different. It's not for sale and he wants it, at least he thinks he wants it. Telling a man like Forrest Jennings that something isn't for sale makes him want it."

"So he has it stolen and finds a way to protect it."

"The wall was a pretty good trick, you have to admit," Spivey said, braking hard for the railroad tracks near the bottom of Thirty-first Street.

"So he gets the car protected and then lets a few people know he has it," Alton said.

"Well, a few people *do* know and our client is one of them. But this is a car you have to see to even believe it exists."

"You think the auction is a phony? Just his way of showing it off to a select group of people?"

"I assure you, Mr. Franklin, that we're taking the auction very seriously. Stealing the car is simply a contingency plan. Our commission is based on the price the car earns at auction should your bid be too low."

He turned into a small building that looked no larger than a toll booth on the turnpike. Only this building was constructed in the side of a steep, rocky hill. Within a hundred yards, they were underground, inside the electrically lighted streets carved out of Kansas City's famous limestone caverns. The caves were used for storage. Because of the year-round cool temperatures, the federal government stored tons of commodity cheese in the facility.

Except for the stone walls dripping ground water, it looked pretty much like any crammed warehouse district with narrow streets. But to Alton, driving through the caverns felt something like a ride in a theme park. It was spooky and the air always smelled of auto and truck exhaust, though Alton knew there must be fans somewhere to circulate fresh air.

There were the usual loading docks and delivery trucks. There was even a small number of public businesses in the caves, including a large car rental outfit with a showroom in Westport. The dark corners of the underground storage park added a dismal gloom to Alton's $200,000 enterprise that he hadn't anticipated.

Spivey pulled into a slot in front of a wide aluminum door that had been painted with the number 38. The bare light bulb over the door reflected in the young blond's wire-rim glasses as the attorney pressed a remote-control and the door cranked slowly up. Their headlights illuminated a storage unit forty feet deep and twelve feet wide. Cardboard cartons lined one side wall of the short tunnel.

He pushed the button again and the door began to close. They waited till it banged shut before speaking.

"That's it. I leave it here with the keys in it and walk?"

"We'd prefer you didn't use accomplices, naturally. And, of course, you won't be followed."

"Of course," Alton said, plotting.

"Then you pick up your money and leave town," Spivey said, staring at the glare on the windshield.

"And how will you know the car's here?"

"Oh, I'll be here when you bring it in," Spivey said. He turned in his seat to face Alton. "You'll call and let me know when that will be. We're not paying you to play games with us, Mr. Franklin."

Alton bit back a string of acerbic comments, then spoke carefully, fixing Spivey with his own intense stare.

"In which case, it's time you tell me about the car."

Spivey glanced anxiously away. "I suppose you're right," he began reluctantly, as if giving up the family secret that involved ancestral incest and illicit births.

"Well?" Alton prodded.

"Ray said you'd want to know, but let me tell you right

now it would be better if you didn't." Spivey spoke rapidly, rushing his words. "I wish you'd just take my word for it. There's a chance you won't be shown the car. There's a chance you won't have to or may not be able to steal it for us, in which case . . ."

"Cut the horseshit," Alton firmly interrupted.

"No one will believe you even if you do tell them," Spivey said softly, trying it seemed to reassure himself. "I'm not even certain that I believe it."

"It's just a crummy car!" Alton finally exploded. "You act like you're talking about a nuclear bomb wrapped in Joan of Arc's underwear."

Spivey appeared mostly unaffected by the outburst, though his left hand twitched nervously on the steering wheel. He'd be good in court, Alton thought, as long as he kept his hands hidden.

"It's the SS 100 X."

Alton waited. Was that supposed to mean something?

"What's that?" he asked. "Elvis' Camaro, a Datsun, some sort of sports car?"

"It's a 1961 Lincoln convertible. Customized, dark blue."

Alton tried to picture it. No matter how it was painted, a '61 Lincoln Continental in his mind came out looking square and boring, a box on wheels.

"A presidential limousine, Mr. Franklin."

On the drive back to the Alameda, where Alton had booked two rooms, keeping the second room secret from even Monique, James Spivey brought up something new.

"The girl," Spivey said as they slid by the fountains fringing the Country Club Plaza. "I can't advise it really, but you might consider taking her tomorrow night. Just in case the auction's for real."

"Actually, I wasn't going to tell her anything."

"That's not a bad idea, keeping her in the dark about this." Spivey turned the sedan into the covered parking garage behind the Alameda Plaza Hotel instead of dropping off Alton at the lobby entrance. "It's just that, well, Jennings is said to have a certain weakness."

"Bubbly brunettes with big tits?" Alton guessed.

"Women," Spivey said. "All sizes, all shapes, preferably young."

Alton wasn't totally unfamiliar with that particular weakness himself. Spivey looked for a parking slot briefly, then gave up and put it in park in the middle of the driving lane.

"And there really isn't anyone she could tell who would believe her?"

"I suppose not." Since learning that the car was inside the Jennings mansion, Alton had been considering his alternatives and, while his shopping list was far from complete, there was one thing he was certain of.

"I need a pickup truck," he told the young attorney.

Spivey looked as if he were going to protest, thinking no doubt that Alton had plenty of up-front money to cover his own expenses.

"I'd suggest renting it under a name that can't be traced," Alton added before Spivey could speak. "If you can't figure out how to do that, you might buy a used one outright. But not from a dealer. Read the want ads and give some guy what he's asking. Have him hand over the title and pay cash."

"Perhaps I should wear a disguise during the purchase?"

"Now you're catching on. Or have a flunky buy it for you."

"I see," Spivey said blandly. "And when do you need this truck?"

"Tomorrow morning, early," Alton emphasized. "And make sure the damn thing starts."

"Speaking of which, we'll have your bid ready for you

tomorrow morning. It will be accompanied by a very legitimate letter of credit made out in your name and drawn on a San Francisco bank."

Alton had the car door open. He waited while a small foreign car squealed around the parked sedan and made its impatient way between the rows of parked cars in the garage.

"How much?" he asked.

"Thirteen-point-five," Spivey said. "And we have our fingers crossed it will be high bid."

It took Alton a second to comprehend that he meant *million.*

"For a tenth of that," Alton said, "you could have Ford Motor Company and whoever else was involved make you one just like it." He pushed the car door fully open and climbed out.

"It wouldn't be the same," Spivey called after him.

Alton parked his van on a side street lined with cheesy apartment buildings in Kansas City's midtown red-light district and led Monique around the corner onto Main. They walked around two overdressed girls on the sidewalk and past Ray's Playpen, an adult video arcade and standard American dirty-book store.

"Where are you taking me?"

"I used to live here," Alton said, walking, taking in the details that really hadn't changed in the past three years.

"Yeah, I bet," Monique giggled. "If you make me look at strippers, I'll get even, Frankie. I swear."

Alton didn't need nudity. He needed a place to think. One of the decisions he had to make shortly was whether to involve Monique in the auction. The auction itself, he thought, should be safe. Of course he wouldn't let her know a thing about actually stealing the car. And that little criminal act, he realized, would have to be quick. If someone else's bid was accepted, the car would need to be relocated as soon as possible. He wondered how long it took brick masons to tear down a mansion wall.

He held open the inner door of Milton's and ushered Monique in ahead of him, giving his eyes time to adjust to the darkness.

There was a trick he'd learned for entering darkened lounges and movie theaters, along with other pitch-black businesses closed for the night. It was as simple as winking one eye on the outside and keeping it closed till you were inside. Then you shut your other eye, the winked eye fully adjusted to the darkness suddenly surrounding you. It was so simple, it worked. It was so simple, he often forgot to use it.

The place wasn't the same without Milton Morris sitting on a bar stool at the tall table in front of the door, a foot-long cigar in his mouth, greeting you as you walked in with some line straight from the Kansas City Jazz Age like "What's cookin', cats?"

A couple shadows hunched over drinks at the bar to one side of the room. Taking Monique by the arm, Alton stepped down into the main floor of the club, which was empty this early in the evening. The room was dimly lighted by design.

The original yellowed walls were four inches in back of a false wall of pasteboard painted black. Highly stylized shapes of horns and other musical instruments had been cut into the black pasteboard of the false wall. Light fixtures between the old yellow wall and the pasteboard cast pale gold illumination through the cutouts, like music itself hesitatingly lighting the room.

The back room, through which you walked to the rest rooms, was similarly done, only high along the rear wall were framed black-and-white glossies of Milton in his prime, of Milton Morris with the Bird, Gillespie, and Basie. There were pictures, too, of faces you couldn't recognize. Only a concentrated study of the corner autographs would reveal the identities of Lawrence Denton,

Eddie Barefield, Sam Price, Duke Lankford and even more obscure performers in the wide-open town Kansas City had once been.

The tables were small, heavy squares, the seats low. Black, plastic couches lined the walls. You sat where you wanted and brought the table up close.

"Talk about strippers," Alton mused, laying his head against the back of the plastic couch, "used to be a place downtown called the Chesterfield Club. It was a businessmen's spot. And it featured nude waitresses, always four. Two were white and two were black. And they had their pubic hair shaved into the shape of a heart, a diamond, a club and a spade."

"You used to go there?" Monique asked, wiggling to get comfortable on the couch, caught between leaning primly forward on her knees or lounging back against the cushion.

"No way," Alton laughed. "It was the late twenties, early thirties. Milton told me about it."

"Milton?"

"Milton Morris. This is his place."

"I see. You mean like in history?"

"Atmosphere," Alton sighed, unable to explain. He pushed his head further back and stared at the black ceiling. It was like trying to look into a bottomless pit when you wanted to find sky.

"He always ran this ad in the Personals," Alton continued. "Said, *I Ain't Mad at Nobody.* Ran that ad for decades."

"I don't get it," Monique said, smiling in the dim light, a shadow of flute across her face.

"Say you wrote a bad check, you were welcome back. Or maybe you had a little loan or hadn't paid the bar tab, stuff like that."

"How about you?" Monique asked. "Are you mad at somebody?"

"Used to be," Alton said thoughtfully. "I'm not sure anymore."

"No? I thought maybe you were mad at me for being along."

Alton looked at her, her dark, wide eyes, her full mouth. "I didn't mean to make you feel that way. I've got a little business to do here and I guess I'm a little distracted."

That was enough for Monique. She smiled warmly at Alton, then glanced away, listening to the music coming out of the speakers. Life was like that when you were twenty-three, Alton thought, and troubles were easy to fix. He sat up.

On weekends there was a stand-up combo, but Milton had been known for his vintage-jazz record collection and two of the best bass-playing speakers ever constructed by mankind. Requests for particular artists were politely ignored while the bartender put on one album after another, working his way through the entire collection that took months to exhaust, then starting over again.

Someone Alton was at a loss to recognize pushed a tenor sax through an unknown bluesy number that sounded deliciously improvised, if a wee evil.

"A mint julep," Monique requested of the cocktail waitress when she slid two cardboard coasters across the square, slate table. The intent of her order wasn't lost on Alton.

"We can do the julep, honey," the woman said, "but we're fresh out of mint leaves."

"That's fine," Monique chirped cheerfully. The waitress rolled her eyes toward Alton and he decided on a bottled beer. Tomorrow was going to be a big day and he needed to stay away from the scotch.

"In a couple days we'll be in Louisville," Alton was saying. "I'll help you handicap, I promise."

"I know. You've always been considerate about things.

You're the nicest gambler I've ever met. I just don't know what we're doing here, Frankie, while the horses are there."

"Taking a breather, that's all. A little breather. You know, I've actively avoided this town for nearly three years and it feels good to be back here. I wouldn't call it home or anything like that, but it feels kind of good."

"But what if all the jobs are gone by the time I get around to the clubs in Louisville? And I won't be able to get in on the backup list at the track. You know that all the concession jobs go to the locals and we have to fill in where we can."

"I'll get you something. I know a couple places here and there."

Monique wasn't pleased; but she trusted him.

"Who knows? Maybe you'll win enough not to have to work," Alton added for good measure.

Their drinks came, the music changed to piano, and Alton filled her in on Tuesday night. He said they would be going to a small, formal party.

"I'll be honest with you, Monique, the guy giving the party has a reputation as a womanizer and it would help if you flirted a little."

"Is that all?" Monique asked, openly suspicious.

"You'll be with me," he promised. "I'm your date. It would help if this guy likes us is all."

"Is he fat?" Monique wanted to know.

"I have no idea; but he's rich."

"Well, if he's fat, you owe me one."

CHAPTER FOUR

Tuesday morning, Alton was dressed and shaved before Monique awakened. The excitement was there, crouched inside him and ready to spring. He felt much as he felt on the mornings when he'd discovered a juicy horse the night before in the *Daily Form.* Alton Franklin wanted to steal the car, not to buy it. But for the time being this was a secret he kept from even himself. Nothing got the blood going on an early morning like planning the theft of a $13.5 million car.

Alton was pleased that this particular car theft was tactically challenging, though he pretended that he wouldn't have to go through with it. Who the hell would turn down $13.5 million for a car? He sat on the edge of the bed and, bending over, nuzzled Monique's sleep-warm neck. Her skin smelled of baby oil and shampoo.

There was something about this girl he liked. Perhaps it was her innate pleasure with life. Monique Rene Wolfert was a person who'd draw a red circle around a green stain on the wall and call it Christmas.

Monique purred, but wouldn't open her eyes. He kissed her then and nibbled. Eventually her arm lifted from the covers, revealing her full breasts, and she wrapped it around his neck. She attempted to pull Alton back into bed. Alton resisted and spoke loudly, a stern father laying down the rules for a rebellious child.

"I have to run some errands today," he said as her dark, wide eyes blinked open. Monique grimaced at the light. "You'll be on your own. I left some money on the dresser. Why don't you go shopping and buy something nice for tonight?"

He was standing now.

"Okay," she mumbled. Monique massaged a palm against her face, furrowing her brow. "Where?"

"Across the street, just walk over to the Plaza."

Kansas City's Country Club Plaza was considered the Rodeo Drive of the Midwest, with fourteen blocks of Spanish-style shops and restaurants, complete with towers, balconies and courtyards. Many of the world's most exclusive shops lived there, from Gucci's to Bonwit Teller to Neiman Marcus. There were enough fountains in the Plaza to drown the entire Mormon Tabernacle Choir. Those who survived might enjoy risking their lives taking a horse-drawn carriage, another popular feature of the ritzy shopping district.

"Okay." Monique abandoned the idea of being awake and slipped down under the covers. Rolling over on her side, she drew up her legs to form a cocoon of warmth.

"And remember, darling, something nice. It's formal."

Monique moaned softly what might have been a reply. It was possible she was fully asleep. It was possible, Alton thought, she was dreaming a winner. If winners were dreamed from juleps and jazz.

He checked at the desk for messages and was given a large orange envelope. It contained, along with his promised letter of credit and other papers, a set of car keys and a scrawled note that told him the keys fit a 1976 Ford pickup, green. He located the truck in the covered parking facility, then returned to his van for gloves.

Behind the wheel, he surveyed the papers Spivey had included in his packet. Setting aside his invitation to the auction, Alton read a poorly photocopied Ford Motor Company news release dated June 14, 1961, the day the SS 100 X was delivered to the White House.

Delivery of the new Presidential Continental is the culmination of four years of planning and discussion with the Secret Service.

The navy blue limousine has more specially designed features and accessories than any automobile ever used for official duties at the White House. Major innovations include a series of roof combinations, a rear seat that can be raised and lowered automatically, retractable foot stands for Secret Service men, two-way radio telephones and a master control panel for power accessories.

The President can ride in the car in the open air, either sitting or standing. Assuring protection in all types of weather and for various conditions, the President also can ride under a metal roof, a transparent plastic roof or a convertible top.

Alton wondered briefly if *all types of weather* included times when it rained bullets from schoolbook depositories. So far, he was discovering nothing noted that would make this car more difficult to steal than any other 1961 Continental. You could hot-wire most cars from the early sixties without using your thumbs.

The car, which is more than 21 feet in overall length, is an elongated version of the 1961 Lincoln Continental convertible. It was designed by Ford Motor Company technicians in cooperation with Hess & Eisenhardt, a custom-body firm in Cincinnati, Ohio.

The car is divided into two compartments with a power-operated sliding glass partition separating the driver compartment from the passengers. The rear passenger area includes two folding jump seats and a backseat that can accommodate comfortably three people.

But not if they're carrying roses, Alton thought, a sudden picture of the young First Lady flashed through his mind, surprising Alton. He hadn't quite realized that the television news coverage of the assassination was such a permanent part of his visual memory. A shiver tickled the back of his neck.

A unique feature of the car is the power-operated backseat, which can be raised to a height of $10^1/_2$ inches from the floor when the rear roof section is removed. The adjustable seat, which has foot steps for maximum comfort, permits the President to be seen easily even though seated.

The rest of the release was a list of interior accessories that included mouton carpet, light blue and matching dark blue leather, and two lap robes each embroidered with the presidential seal. There was some discussion of the transparent plastic roof that came in six sections, each of which was removable. Along with the three-section convertible top, the plastic bubble-top could be stored in the trunk.

They don't make trunks like they used to.

A black "formal" roof of metal was manufactured in two sections. The passenger section was outfitted with a small rectangular window. When transported outside the Washington, D.C., area, this roof was crated separately.

At the rear of the car is a Continental spare-tire design, which is partially recessed into the trunk lid. Two foot stands are built into the rear bumper. Detachable grip handles are mounted into the trunk lid area.

Alton distinctly remembered those handles on the trunk lid. Had it been from the television pictures or photographs in the newspaper? He also recalled that no one had been riding the rear bumper at the time the rifle shots were fired into the backseat from a window of the brick warehouse in Dallas.

All in all, the car wasn't worth 13.5 million. Perhaps his bid would win the auction. He wondered absently if the SS 100 X, like Winston Churchill's Rolls-Royce, had been outfitted with cigar-size ashtrays.

Alton removed a handful of disposable latex gloves from a gross-box he'd stored in one of the small cabinets of the converted van. It was important he left no fingerprints on the Ford pickup because he planned to leave it behind. It was his design that when he left the scene of the crime, were there to be a crime, he'd be driving a twenty-one-foot limousine.

Renting a tuxedo was last on his list. A forty-two-long off the rack fit his six-foot frame as well as anything he'd ever had tailored. Something they had in stock would have to do. Alton reminded himself that he also needed an appropriate pair of shoes.

Stops included purchases at a hardware store and hobby shop in the Ward Parkway Shopping Center. A floor salesclerk in a department store gave him the name and address of a fellow who dealt in used lawn mowers. Alton wanted at least two. And a manageable wheelbarrow would come in handy. He already knew the location of a midtown hunting-supply shop that sold reloading paraphernalia.

Alton used a dish towel he'd bought at the department store to open and close the door to climb into and out of the truck. He drove with a pair of the thin rubber gloves stretched over his hands. Driving across town to look up someone he knew on Thirty-ninth Street, Alton winked at the fifty-pound sack of fertilizer he'd loaded onto the passenger floorboard of the green Ford pickup.

"You and me against them," he said to the fertilizer. "Two sacks of shit out to do better for themselves."

Alton was awash with the same giddy arousal that overcame him when he was on his way to the window to lay a heavy bet on the nose of a horse he'd never seen run before.

The sack of fertilizer was chosen because it was the brand with the highest nitrogen content. It would do just fine for the bit of gardening he had in mind.

CHAPTER FIVE

Monique came dressed as a new flavor of birthday cake. She wore peach-tinted pantyhose in patterned lace under a striking orange and white polka-dot dress, the white circles the size of ice cream scoops. Twin half circles of stiffened cloth appeared wholly inadequate to contain the ample servings of her milky breasts, the buoyancy of which were unaffected by the dress. You wouldn't have to turn her upside down for most of Monique Rene Wolfert to spill out of her dress.

The mini length of the full skirt appeared to be starched, or held up by wires, floating horizontally out from her narrow waist. Monique's creamy complexion had been adapted by makeup to match the outfit. Her hair remained raven. Alton was happy to see she hadn't dyed it orange for the event. As they glided under a streetlight he quickly checked to make sure her eyes were still deep brown. They were, and they gleamed with excitement. Women love parties—especially when they get to wear new clothes.

She also wore a bracelet of what appeared to be tiny marshmallows around one wrist. Matching marshmallows swung on silverware from either delicate ear. It was a sweet getup.

Though they'd arrived on time, even to the point of waiting in the taxi a few minutes out front before approaching the door, it seemed as if they'd come late. A man in tails, looking as much like a penguin as a pianist, ushered them into a large sitting room already peopled with other guests. Perhaps their arrivals had been purposefully staggered by their host, Alton considered, scrutinizing the rooms, trying to get a feel for the layout of the walls, the doorways.

"Mr. Alton Franklin," their tailed escort announced to the parlor before beating a hasty retreat.

"I'm Monique," she said cheerfully at his side to the others gathered in the room. An Asian man with large eyes nodded primly in her direction. He stood nervously in a corner of the large room, as if waiting in line to use the men's room.

An older man, complete with white hair and the kind of rosy cheeks Alton associated with Santa Claus, lifted his glass to the two of them from his casual command of a Hepplewhite settee. Something in the twinkle of his eyes told Alton he was the type of man who could gut you with his penknife without getting blood on his cuff or his shoes.

A woman in a shimmery white evening gown and diamonds stood beside an ornately carved side table. She inspected a painting on the wall with some private amusement. No doubt she could do better. There was a flash of emerald and diamond from the side of her face as she turned her back upon the most recently arrived guests.

"She must think it's her best side," Monique whispered to Alton with distaste.

A tall black man leaned against a perfectly polished grand piano. He flicked cigarette ashes into a crystal bowl and except for that, and the fact his eyes were open, he might have been asleep. All told it wasn't a rowdy crowd. Despite the older man's apparent joviality, Alton felt as if he'd just stepped into a freezer.

For $100,000, Alton could tolerate the chill. A Mozart flute concerto wafted into the room from points unknown. Jennings must have a CD jukebox in the rumpus room of the kitchen, Alton kidded himself. It was more likely the Hanoverian Orchestra itself was warming up in the backyard.

You'd think, if you were spending millions, there'd at least be someone there doing magic tricks, telling jokes. What was provided instead was a bartender, who stood before them, holding a silver tray, waiting.

"Coffee," Alton said.

"Do you have champagne?" Monique asked.

He nodded, then said to Alton, "Your bid, sir."

Alton reached inside his tuxedo jacket and removed a sealed envelope, feeling the eyes of the other four bidders upon him, their expressions unchanged. He placed the envelope on the tray and battled back the desire to shout, *"Thirteen-point-five, can you top it?"*

"And a scotch," he said instead, not looking at the bartender, bid-taker. "Rocks."

"Of course, sir."

"Are you buying a horse?" Monique asked out of the corner of her painted mouth and giggled, already tipsy with the idea of champagne.

"Something like that."

A small squeak of delight escaped from Monique's throat and she turned to smile broadly upon the room. Alton shuffled his eyes among the other players. The white-haired gentleman on the settee smiled back at Monique. She'd have fun in a train wreck, Alton thought. Actually, he'd seen merrier crowds in intensive-care waiting rooms.

"Is that him?" Monique asked, leaning back toward Alton, gesturing slightly toward jolly ol' St. Nick. Alton shook his head, certain Forrest Jennings was waiting to make an entrance.

The bartender, or whatever he was, brought them their drinks and Alton ended up with a cup and saucer in one hand, a glass in the other. Alton's scotch came in a small water glass, ice cubes stacked mistakenly to the brim. He had to bang the ice against his face to suck the liquor out.

Monique daintily accepted her bubbly in good spirit. Alton was afraid she might curtsy. Together, they watched the servant carry the tray and place it, with the silver ice bucket cradling Monique's *blanc de blancs,* on the narrow table next to the woman in white. She ignored him with obvious contempt.

There might be further bidders yet to arrive, Alton knew. Eventually he made his way to the painting and the woman in white, while Monique took up temporary residence on the Hepplewhite, having difficulty with her skirt as she sat. He heard the low mumble of the older man's conversation with Monique and, at one point, thought he heard her cheerily say, "Oh, we play the horses."

The painting was an eighteenth-century boatscape darkened with age. The woman's eyes were the same color of green as the emeralds centered in her diamond earrings, her hair as dark as Monique's and somehow more silken. Her perfume engulfed him as she began her slow but deliberate move away from Alton and the gilded frame on the wall with a sideways look that could put a limp in rocketships.

He should have felt like a brand-new species of fungus. Instead, he was intrigued. There was something about this woman that told him she was trying very hard to fit into a world in which she did not belong. He pretended her disdainful arrogance was a con.

Alton sat his coffee cup and saucer on the carved table and gave chase. Feigning to concentrate his attention on the furnishings and the wall, he took two casual sideways steps each time she took one. Of course, he'd have to step on her foot to get her to look at him; but even that wasn't out of the question. Besides, there was a pair of sliding oak doors at the end of the room he wanted to investigate.

The black man ignited another cigarette. The Asian paced inside his skin, his eyes constantly darting.

One step from Alton's brushing elbows with her, she stopped. And, without quite looking at him, the green-eyed beauty said, "That's quite enough. I didn't come here to *meet* people."

At least she considered him people, Alton thought.

"Thirteen-point-five," he said quickly, before she could move away. Take that! Her expression revealed no reaction at all and once again she turned her back on him. As the woman in white strode purposefully across the plush Oriental carpet, perhaps to explore the wall on the other side of the room, Alton watched her go with an unhidden stare of animal appreciation. It *was* her best side, he concluded.

The white-haired man had walked comfortably to the carved table and had returned to the settee with Monique's silver bucket of champagne by the time Alton had reached the double doors. The SS 100 X might be sitting on the other side. Of all the bidders in the room, Alton could only imagine himself driving it.

The long Lincoln would easily fit through the double doorway, but then there'd be no way out of this room. Unless someone moved the piano, there was no way the limousine could cross the room, for that matter.

Alton stood behind the settee, his glass empty, when the little party was startled by the opening of the oak doors. The pink-cheeked older man stood and Monique followed suit, her marshmallow earrings swinging. Everyone turned to watch Jennings stride into the room. The tall, thin man came to a stop between the Hepplewhite and the grand piano to address the gathering.

"I'm quite pleased," he announced perfunctorily, "that each of you was able to attend this evening." He paused, holding the pipe before him like a wand. There was a definite gleam in his eye, an energy. Jennings had prepared for this moment: He was a consummate actor.

"Mr. Franklin, did you think there'd be dancing?" he asked haughtily, looking directly at Monique instead of Alton. No one promised Alton that Jennings would be likable.

"I'm Monique Wolfert," she said.

"And I'm Forrest Jennings. I do hope you enjoy your visit to my home."

Before she could reply, Jennings was addressing the room again in a new tone of seriousness. "Mr. Soo," he called, as if uncertain where Mr. Soo might be standing. "You may pick up your coat at the door."

The Asian took a quick step forward upon hearing his name, then froze. "I . . . I don't understand . . ."

"Your bid has been rejected, sir. Please inform your associates that I have no interest in doing business with them now or at any time in the future."

"No," the small man sputtered. "It's not . . ."

"Fair?" Jennings asked. "Few things are, Mr. Soo. Your offer to best the top bid by a million dollars wasn't even considered. You see, I don't do business with leeches."

Monique giggled at the tall man's polished formality and name-calling. Jennings drew his pipe in against his narrow chest and waited for Mr. Soo to stamp across the room. The Asian turned in the entryway as if to say something, abruptly changed his mind, and was followed out of the room by the bartender, who, Alton noticed, had kept his hand inside his jacket throughout the interchange between Soo and Jennings.

"And then there were four," Jennings said with a chuckle. He placed the pipe in his mouth and, allowing the remaining members of the party to peek at his diamond cuff links, he adjusted his cuffs with either manicured hand in turn. They matched the diamond studs in his shirt, Alton noted.

The bartender-butler-bodyguard reappeared in the entryway, which was Jennings' cue. Act II.

"Now, you will each be so kind as to join me in the

library. Miss Buddery?" Jennings held out an arm toward
the woman in white and Alton saw her smile for the first
time. There was nothing warm about it. Before she could
make her way to accompany Forrest Jennings there was
a commotion at the door that froze everyone in place.

Jennings' man had been grabbed from behind. An arm
was around his neck, ruining his bowtie.

Other uniformed police officers poured into the room,
their guns out, ruining Jennings' performance. They
rushed the tall host, who stood in front of the closed
oaken doors to what Alton guessed was the library.

Monique gasped, thinking it was a raid. Alton knew
better.

The black man slowly sat down on the piano bench, his
broad back to the keys, a burning cigarette held steadily
between two fingers. The woman in white looked rattled, but clung to her surface composure, backed snugly
into the crook of the grand piano. Monique and the
white-haired gentleman stood in front of the settee, with
Alton directly behind them, his hand on the back of the
Hepplewhite.

No one held their hands up, but Alton expected at any
minute to be told to lie on the floor. There were four
uniformed police officers in all, their name tags and
badges tucked safely into their pockets. Jennings' bodyguard was released and shoved toward the piano bench,
the accompanying policeman holding the gun he'd removed from inside the man's dinner jacket in one hand,
his duty revolver in the other. The bartender sat down
indignantly on the bench beside the black man, who
looked up without moving his head.

"I demand to know—" Forrest Jennings began, obviously flustered.

"Shut up!" one of the officers ordered before he could
continue. Jennings brought his pipe down to his side.

Monique seemed calmed by the fact that the men
wore police uniforms, believing that nothing more com-

plicated than an arrest of Forrest Jennings was under way. For her, the party had finally livened up.

But it seemed clear to Alton that a robbery was taking place. It bothered him that the police officers weren't hiding their faces. There was a chance, he believed, they would all be killed. Larger groups of people had been murdered in cold blood for less than a $13.5 million automobile. Except for the music that masked the sound of everyone breathing, the room was silent.

There might as well be Mozart playing when you die, Alton thought.

"Surprise!" A deep voice boomed from the foyer. "It's me!"

A short, portly man in cowboy boots, jeans and a plaid shirt marched into the room with a wooden box under his arm. It was the size and type of box that usually housed silverware. The bald man was smiling madly at Jennings, ignoring the others in the room. He came to a sudden halt on a spot ten paces in front of their host. He was shorter than Forrest Jennings by nearly a foot.

"I've challenged you to a duel and I've chosen the weapons," the party-crasher said. He turned then and motioned the woman in white away from the piano. She moved toward the bench, away from Jennings.

"Nice ass," the fat man said. "Forrest never could resist a piece of ass." One of the police officers coughed as the short man placed the box on top of the piano with a bang. He wore his jeans under a large potbelly in such a manner they appeared as if they'd already fallen off.

"Were you selling it to her?" the fat man asked. He was opening the box. " 'Cause if you were—" he began, then paused to look at the woman in white. " 'Cause if you were, I might reconsider. She wouldn't be bad to negotiate with. Not bad at all."

Leaving the open box on the piano, the bald man spun to face Jennings. His face was scarlet and he was no longer smiling. His gray eyes were small and round and as serious as a gun.

"You stole it from me, Forrest. And I've challenged you and I've chosen the weapons. I suppose it's only fair that you get first shot."

With that, he reached into the box and brought out a silver-and-walnut dueling pistol in each hand.

"You wouldn't," Jennings said breathlessly.

"No?" the fat man asked. "The witnesses? Oh, Forrest, I'm disappointed in you. You of all people should know that witnesses can be bought." He held the guns aloft, pointing straight up.

"Witnesses to what, Forrest? Like I said, you get first shot. I'll be firing in self-defense. Only you and I will know it was a duel and I'm not telling.

"And everyone knows that a dead man hasn't much to say," he added. "Left or right?"

He stared cruelly at the taller man. "Left or right!" he shouted. Everyone, including the police officers tensed.

Alton slipped his hand from the back of the settee, aware that they were present to provide audience for the madman's show. Still, he couldn't quite get comfortable with six guns drawn in the room.

Jennings wasn't talking. Behind his shock there was an anger burning in his eyes. It was perfectly clear that he hated the short, bald man who stamped into his house wearing cowboy boots and jeans to threaten Forrest Jennings' life.

The fat man turned rapidly, riveting in on Monique. He smiled.

"We've never met, darling, have we?"

Monique shook her head no. Alton watched the black man drop his burning cigarette butt into his glass.

"Then you choose for him, sweetie. Left or right?"

It was tougher than picking a horse to bet on. Finally, Monique spoke softly. "Left."

The fat man turned back to face Jennings. "Did you

hear that, Forrest? You have chosen left." With that, he dropped his right hand to his portly side and raised his bushy eyebrows, watching Jennings.

It was just a show, Alton thought. He wasn't going to shoot anybody.

The left gun went off and everybody jumped at the blast.

"You missed," the fat man sang out. "Now it's my turn." He lifted the gun in his right hand to take aim, pointing the long-barreled pistol at Jennings' grimacing face. The uniformed officers backed away from the tall man in his diamonds and tux. Jennings took a faint step backward and found he was against the closed oaken doors. He blanched.

"Should I count to three?" The fat man scowled. "Or just wait till you're through pissing your pants?"

CHAPTER SIX

"Dammit, Harold! You can't!" Jennings shrieked, pleading against the insanity of the situation.

But Harold obviously could. Jennings' emotional collapse was what the fat man had been waiting for. He winked one eye, gritted his teeth, and sighted carefully along his rigid right arm. Jennings' pipe tumbled to the floor. The bald man pulled the trigger.

The shot rang out, hitting an offbeat among the flutes.

Alton flinched and Monique threw her hands to her marshmallowed ears.

Forrest Jennings was hit squarely in the chest. He screamed, his eyes bulging, and jerked his head back, tossing spittle. The tall man clutched at his diamond-studded silk shirt with both hands and slipped to the floor, sliding down the oaken doors. He looked as much like a man who'd suffered a fatal heart attack as someone who'd just been shot by a dueling pistol.

Alton reached across the back of the settee and placed his hands on Monique's shoulders to calm her. He felt an involuntary shudder run through her body, buckling her knees. Monique shook her head from side to side, her eyes closed, but she didn't fall. Monique's response to the shooting was not unlike an orgasm.

The butler-bodyguard was restrained from coming to his employer's assistance. Jennings gasped audibly, raking in air as if to save himself from dying. He had, Alton noticed, wet his trousers. Alton wouldn't have been surprised if his balls had fallen off.

The police officers held their places and, after a moment of triumphant beaming, the fat man lowered his arm and burst out laughing.

The woman in white had turned pale and her mouth was open slightly to take in more air. The black man studied his empty hands.

Jennings rolled over onto the floor. He groaned, still clutching his chest. But there was no blood.

"You're not dead, Forrest." Harold was still chuckling. "The bullet's what you call a dum-dum, dickhead."

A dum-dum was a rubber bullet, Alton knew. And in this case the charge had also been lightened. Alton guessed about half the gunpowder had been emptied from the cartridge. It still made a good pop, but the worst Jennings suffered was a cracked rib and one hell of a hickey on his chest. That, and the fright of his life.

To everyone in the room, though, Forrest Jennings had certainly looked like death on a cracker.

The white-haired man in front of the settee reached for the champagne bottle and filled his glass. Harold replaced both pistols into their wooden box on the piano and then addressed the crowd. His tone was serious but a sly grin played at the corners of his mouth.

"Party's over," he announced. "Your bids have been turned down. The car, you understand, is mine. Don't you agree, Forrest?"

Jennings had pulled himself to a sitting position, his back against the doors, one hand still massaging his shirt. His eyes were red-rimmed and filled with a livid loathing. He chose not to respond to the fat man's pronouncement.

"Barnett will see you to the door," Harold Muleford added. The butler moved away from the piano, glancing back at the crumpled Forrest Jennings, then stepped purposefully toward the entryway.

"One more thing," Harold said as the black man stood from the piano bench and straightened his slacks. "Just in case you think I'm only good for a prank, let me warn

you about that. I own that car and I don't give a damn
whose house it's parked in."

He paused, taking time to look at each of them.

"The car is not for sale and I guard my property jeal-
ously. Those were the last two rubber bullets I'll ever
own."

He turned to the box, adjusted the pistols and closed
the lid.

The woman in white knelt by Forrest Jennings. Her
green eyes were only upon him. It was almost worth
getting shot to have her for a nurse, Alton thought.

In the marble-tiled foyer, the white-haired man with
crisp eyes told Monique it had been nice meeting her.
"And you, Mr. Franklin," he added amiably. His name,
Alton learned, was Rick Feigen.

"May I treat you to an, uh, after-dinner drink in my
suite at Crown Center?"

Monique looked hopeful but Alton declined. He
wasn't interested in going back to Rick's place for a
drink. Alton had other things on his mind, not the least of
which was a fifty-pound bag of fertilizer he'd find something specific to do with early tomorrow morning.

"Perhaps then I can offer the two of you a ride to your
hotel? Miss Wolfert here said you were staying at the
Alameda. It's on the way and it might be we'd have the
opportunity to, uh, discuss pooling our resources?"

Again Alton declined, not at all surprised by Feigen's
suggestion. The fat man had convinced no one to give up
the quest for the SS 100 X.

By the time the taxi Barnett had called for them arrived, everyone but the green-eyed lovely in white had
left the party. Harold and his merry band of hired guns
in police uniforms left in two waiting patrol cars, their
red lights flashing as they screeched out of the drive.

"Rick said they're friends," Monique told Alton, speaking of Harold and Forrest Jennings. "He said they go way
back."

Friends like that shouldn't live in the same country, Alton thought. Harold's hoax was the work of a man who hated his victim. Alton was surprised he hadn't taken a shit on the Oriental carpets.

On the short ride to the Plaza, Monique asked Alton about the car.

"I don't know a damn thing about it," Alton lied. "I was paid to place a bid and then see what happened."

"Was the tall guy with the pipe the one I was supposed to flirt with, Frankie?"

"Somebody beat us to the punch," Alton said, thinking of the woman in white.

"Well, it was a romp, after all." Monique leaned against him in the backseat. "Watching a man get shot is kind of like a roller-coaster ride, Frankie."

Kind of, he thought, like a roller-coaster ride at night when the car leaves the tracks.

Alton had the key to their room at the Alameda and the key to the room across the hall in opposite pockets of his rented dinner jacket. He knew which one to use and held open the door for Monique, allowing plenty of room for her polka-dot skirt to rustle by him and into the room.

The television was on. An unopened bottle of champagne wearing a white-linen stole was in ice on the dresser. Standing next to it was a sealed liter of Johnnie Walker Black and a small plastic tub of melting ice.

"Hello," Monique said cordially, assuming Alton had invited the slight black-haired man in the tuxedo who was standing up from a chair in the corner of the room, smiling broadly.

"I hope you don't mind," Jack Soo said, gesturing with an open hand to the impromptu bar he'd set up on the dresser. Alton noted he kept his other hand inside his jacket pocket. "Perhaps you'd like to relax?"

"Actually, I prefer Red Label," Alton said, stepping

into the room. "I know it costs less and hasn't been aged as long, but I've developed a taste for it."

"Your name is Sue, isn't it?" Monique asked, returning the man's smile tooth for tooth.

"Jack Soo," he said. "Two *o*'s. I'm sorry we weren't properly introduced. You're Monique, are you not? And this is Mr. Franklin."

"That's right," Monique bubbled. "And I'm sorry you had to leave like that. Things were fun right after . . ."

"What do you want?" Alton asked, interrupting Monique's chitchat. Alton hadn't closed the door behind him and considered diving over the threshold as the man pulled his hand from his pocket. He clutched in his fist what might have been a gun.

Alton relaxed only a little as he realized it was the remote-control. Soo pointed it at the television and clicked off the set.

"Call me Jack," the Asian insisted in a precise West Coast accent as Monique plopped down on the edge of the bed to take off her new shoes. "I thought we might talk. That's all. Why don't you shut the door? I'd be happy to fix you a drink."

Alton took one step forward, leaving the door ajar.

"You want to talk, then talk," Alton said. He rested his hand on the end of the dresser.

"Okay, Mr. Franklin. Let me ask you, did you see the car?"

"No. And I don't know anything about it."

"Come now, Mr. Franklin. You wouldn't have been present if . . ."

"I was hired to place a bid," Alton cut him off. "I was told when and where. I was paid in advance. And I'm through. That's everything I know."

"Can we open the champagne now?" Monique looked up as she removed her marshmallow earrings.

"No," Alton said firmly. If Soo were talking in front of Monique he must assume she was in on it. Alton hoped he'd leave her out of the discussion altogether and simultaneously hoped Soo wouldn't reveal too many details. It was bad enough that Rick Feigen had been speaking to her.

Monique faked a huge frown and lay back on the bed, rebuffed. Her orange skirt popped up as she did so, but Monique didn't seem to mind. Soo glanced at her legs, then turned to give Alton the once-over. He was no longer smiling.

"And you have no idea who was paying the gentleman who hired you?"

"Absolutely none."

"This James Spivey works for Sargent Security. Do you think Mr. Sargent was attempting to buy the car?"

Alton said nothing.

"A client then?"

Again Alton was mute, his face without expression.

"You see, Mr. Franklin, I, too, was hired to place a bid. Only I know who I am working for. And we are still very interested in procuring this automobile. We know quite a few things about the car and we know quite a few things about the other bidders. You, for instance . . . this room."

That was a piece of cake. They'd had Spivey tailed. Alton's name was announced at the auction.

Soo's mood changed abruptly, no longer playing games. "The point is we very strongly doubt that you were hired merely to place a bid, Mr. Franklin. Or should I call you Rooster?"

Alton tensed.

"You possess a certain history we are aware of, a history, shall we say, that would make your services desirable to one who wanted to possess the car without following through on their bid. That's why my people offered to top all bids tonight. And the point, Mr. Franklin, is that we're still very willing to pay for the car."

Monique drummed her fingers on the bed, losing patience.

"We know what you're up to, Franklin," Soo said, beginning to pace in front of the sitting table. "We know exactly what you're up to. She was going to keep Mr. Jennings busy and you were going to drive off with his most prized possession."

Soo spoke rapidly, without pausing.

"Now, I've received a report that the auction was interrupted by the arrival of the police. We don't care about that. But we're convinced you are still planning to take the car."

"People have been wrong about me before," Alton said.

"But we're not wrong." Soo paused to calm himself, tried on a thin smile and then continued. "I must return to Las Vegas tonight. But my people have business associates in Kansas City who can be trusted.

"We want that car very badly, and we're offering a two-million-dollar finder's fee. A man could live a lifetime on two million dollars, Mr. Franklin."

Monique stiffened. She blinked, her eyes widening as she looked from Alton to Jack Soo and back again.

Soo reached into his jacket pocket and produced a pen. He turned to the table and began to write on a piece of Alameda stationery lying next to his empty glass.

"I'm leaving you a phone number, Mr. Franklin. It's a local call. You call this number should you find the car and we'll see to it that two million dollars are at your personal disposal upon delivery."

"Frankie," Monique said in a hushed voice. "Two million dollars."

Soo spun on his well-polished heels and smiled briefly at her. He nodded politely to Alton as he walked by him toward the open door. There, he turned again.

"My associates certainly don't mind paying two million dollars for the car, Mr. Franklin. It's a drop in the bucket. But I can assure you, we would be extremely upset with you and your girlfriend here if you were to find the car and turn it over to anyone else."

He added, "Drinks are on me." Then Jack Soo closed the door behind him.

"Shitfire!" Monique exclaimed, jumping up from the bed. "Do you know where this car is, Frankie? Do you?"

Alton stepped around her to the sitting table, picked up Soo's glass and smelled it. Just as Alton thought, the man had been sipping water.

"Well!" Monique demanded, her hands on her hips, bunching her skirt.

"Well," Alton said, eyeing the twenty-four-ounce jar of sweet gherkins on the bedside stand. "You want another pickle?" There were still several in the jar and Alton wanted it empty by morning.

"I certainly do not," she huffed. Monique reached over and grabbed the bottle of *blanc de blancs* that perfectly matched the bottle she'd been served at the Jennings mansion. "Pickles don't go well with champagne. And neither do you."

With that, Monique marched into the bathroom, where moments later, Alton heard the pop of the iced champagne being opened. *Shitfire* was right, he thought. Alton had a couple million things to consider before going to sleep.

He opened the jar of gherkins and forced himself to eat one. Two million dollars would cover just about any losing streak Alton could come up with in his worst nightmare. Money had always been Alton's blind spot. That, and fancy women in shimmering evening gowns.

CHAPTER SEVEN

Alton Franklin woke early, remembering that he'd heard her name. Jennings had called her Miss Buddery. He washed out the pickle jar and dried it with an Alameda towel. He left Monique a note, asking her to stay close by today and to talk to no one about anything that happened last night.

He considered calling the young attorney who worked for Ray Sargent, then decided against it. It wasn't like a thief to tip his hand to anybody. And, in truth, Alton wasn't certain yet who he was working for. It could be a $100,000 job or it could be a $2 million job. Either way, it was clear to him his personal safety was at risk. Working for Jack Soo was, in fact, about twenty times riskier than handing the car over to James Spivey. Still, it was a gamble Alton hadn't quite decided to pass on.

A wise man might have settled for the $100,000 he'd already been paid to place the bid. But Alton had never considered himself a wise man. Besides, he *wanted* to steal that car. If for no other reason than to keep the fat man named Harold from having it.

And Alton somehow wanted the elusive Miss Buddery to think highly of him.

It wasn't quite dawn as Alton crawled into the back of his van in the Alameda parking garage. He tugged on a pair of latex gloves and, using a screwdriver, pounded a small hole into the jar lid. He unrolled about eighteen inches of the waterproof fuse he'd bought at the hobby shop. The fuse was sold to model-rocket enthusiasts.

He threaded the fuse through the hole, then knotted it

so it wouldn't slip back out through the hole in the lid. Alton removed the sealed can of gunpowder he'd bought at the reloading supplies counter and filled the jar with the shiny black-silver dots. The jar still smelled of pickle brine as he screwed on the lid, forcing about six inches of the fuse down into the gunpowder.

Alton used to like sweet gherkins. Now, he figured it would be several months before he could bring himself to eat another one.

After placing the jar of fused gunpowder into a shopping bag, Alton changed into his new set of khakis and pulled on a pair of clean, white sneakers. He felt like a Boy Scout without merit badges. He put on a Royals cap he'd purchased along with the rest of his new outfit.

Carrying his package of pickle jar and fuse to the green Ford pickup, Alton was pleased to see that no one had bothered the three beat-up lawn mowers and the rusty blue wheelbarrow in the bed of the truck.

Still wearing his gloves, the fingertips darkened with gunpowder, Alton rattled toward Fifty-fifth Street and the Jennings estate. The sun had popped up to see what was happening as Alton parked just inside the long driveway off Fifty-fifth.

His adrenaline surging, Alton hoped he looked like a lawn-care worker getting an early start on a Wednesday morning in April. A passerby would have to look very closely to notice he wore a different kind of glove. There was more traffic than he'd anticipated at this hour, but most of the cars buzzed along Ward Parkway, which ran past the east side of the estate. Alton was pleased the house hadn't been built close to the street.

He loaded the fertilizer into the blue wheelbarrow, placed his pickle jar still in its sack alongside. His load looked nothing like a nitrogen bomb. Anxious to get it done, Alton pushed it hurriedly up the drive, toward the recently re-bricked west side of the mansion. It seemed to Alton that the few cars driving on Fifty-fifth Street at his back were full of good citizens taking in every detail of his early morning romp so they could later finger him for the police.

He set the jar into the crook of the fireplace on the outside wall, careful that the jar of powder was placed upside down. There was a very, *very* slight chance that, if the jar were upright, the hole through the lid would provide enough air for the gunpowder to flash-burn rather than explode. It was a chance, though, that when you were making a bomb you didn't dare to take.

Alton unloaded the sack of high-nitrogen fertilizer atop the jar, tamping it down with his foot.

The horses had reached the starting gate. Alton wanted to wash his sweaty hands. He unrolled all twelve feet of fuse. That done, he absentmindedly rubbed gunpowder residue into his right eye. Everything itched.

Ready to get his bang-up head start on the Fourth of July, Alton cursed, remembering at the last moment the one thing he'd forgotten. He didn't have a match.

Leaving the wheelbarrow on the side-yard lawn, he trotted back down to the pickup. Jerking open the passenger door, he grabbed the small paper sack on the floorboard and tore mercilessly at the blister-pack housing a disposable lighter. He finally got the damn thing out of its package and discovered his breath was heavily labored after jogging back to the wall. Gardeners don't run, he told himself.

But then gardeners don't usually set off homemade bombs. He ignited the fuse and hightailed it to the carriage house. Panting, Alton waited around the corner of the smaller brick building, his back against the wall. It was cool enough so he could see his breath rise in small, evaporating clouds as time took its own sweet time to happen.

What if Barnett came out to see what was going on? What if that sack of shit blew down the whole stupid house? What if it blew a big hole in the ground and left the bricks perfectly intact? What if the SS 100 X was parked behind the other fireplace? What if the gas tank was empty? What if Alton's mom found out? And what if the rig didn't go off in the first place?

"How the hell long does it take for a dumb-ass piece of fuse to burn itself up?" Alton worried aloud.

He needn't have worried. The neighborhood was shaken. Alton's Ward Parkway wake-up call rattled windows in the Alameda Plaza Hotel itself. He heard the twisted wheelbarrow slam into one of the aluminum garage doors of the converted carriage house in the midst of the deafening blast. Alton had bet on a horse named Jericho. And the wall came tumbling down.

For a moment, Alton stood in place and stared at the large, ragged hole in the Jennings mansion. The guys in prison, who'd instructed him in making such a bomb, had told Alton that a sack of high-nitrate fertilizer would take out a small frame house when set off from the inside. He was definitely a believer. The force of this blast, however, had been low and to the outside of the house. It had noisily removed most of the first-story wall, including the fireplace and the foundation, scooping a large, shallow pit in the ground that was littered with bricks.

He had to act fast. No one in the house could still be sleeping. Cars pulled over on Fifty-fifth Street. Dogs from everywhere barked.

Alton skedaddled from his spot, running as if being shot at, crossing the ruined landscape, stumbling over bricks and something else: books. They were everywhere, some torn, others intact. Some were singed, while others smoldered. He'd hit the library; he was sure of that.

Wisps of smoke or dust rose from the savaged ground like ghosts from a graveyard and Alton found it impossible to see inside the ripped-open wall. The sun was on the other side of the house, lifting, and a thick cloud of dust filled the room.

But it was there. Leaping into the room, over the shaved foundation, Alton came to a sudden halt against the front bumper of the SS 100 X. He felt his way around to the driver's side of the limousine, tripped over torn books and bits of Sheetrock. The black cloth top was up on the dark blue convertible that in the shadows looked black to Alton.

The key was in the ignition. Forrest Jennings had placed too much confidence in his wall, his fireplace, his shelves of books. Slamming the door of the big car, he tried the key and the engine started without a hiccup or a hitch.

Nothing in the ravaged room was on fire, Alton thought. He revved the engine and to Alton it sounded like a freight train breaking through the dim echo of the blast. He popped it into gear. The big Lincoln lurched, rolling up what was left of the Oriental carpet on which it had been parked.

All twenty-one feet of the SS 100 X emerged in a flash from the darkened hole and into the pit of scattered bricks and books, into the dusty light of day.

An odd chunk of brick rested against the windshield, which remained unscathed. There was a dent in the hood, though, where the brick had bounced. The small wound caught the morning light and winked at Alton as he tugged his Royals cap low over his eyes with one hand. He raced sideways on the grass, spinning the steering wheel with his other gloved hand to straighten out the 8,000 pounds of thrusting steel that surrounded him.

He never took his foot from the gas.

Two men were dashing up the lawn from the street. Neither had a camera and that was all Alton was concerned about. In two seconds, he flew past the '67 Ford pickup cradling lawn mowers and, his heart leaping, bounced over the sidewalk and the curb. Fishtailing sharply, he gave it more gas. The tires barked as they grabbed pavement.

Something tumbled inside the trunk.

The piece of brick slid away and he hit forty-five miles-an-hour before testing the brakes in preparation for his turn onto State Line Road. Out of sight of the Jennings mansion, Alton slowed to the speed limit, hoping to look like any other limousine out for an early morning wash, on its way to the airport to pick up somebody you'd love to meet.

The twin flags, bearing the seal of the President of the United States, fluttering from standards mounted at the front and to either side of the expansive dark blue hood, were the only giveaway that the car was different. And it was different. The Lincoln had responded to being given the gas like a hemi-outfitted dragster. There was real power contained in the steel box Alton piloted north on State Line Road toward Thirty-ninth Street. Power was something they had not mentioned in the Ford Motor Company news release.

CHAPTER EIGHT

The corner of Thirty-ninth and State Line was now called Jamestown Square. It looked good in the Yellow Pages listings, Alton supposed. He turned right in the big limo, driving back into the Missouri side of Kansas City, catching a windshield of sunlight.

A muscular Hispanic Alton knew only as Meza owned a short block of dilapidated brick storefronts a few blocks in on Thirty-ninth. A small two-story structure on the east end housed Wizards Body Shop, complete with a side lot full of recent wrecks. Meza lived upstairs.

He was the known leader of a motorcycle gang called the Wizards. And the building next to the body shop was given over to the customizing and repair of Harley-Davidsons. The next two storefronts remained vacant, their glass windows fronting Thirty-ninth painted and partially boarded up.

At the west end of the string of bruised structures was a used-clothing store, a boutique operated by Meza's girlfriend. It was, among other things, an outlet for buying stolen goods. If you wanted Meza, you had to go into the boutique and ask. Alton had sold his share of booty in years past over the counter of the boutique.

After his shopping spree Tuesday morning, Alton had dropped by and paid the motorcyclist and Jamestown Square entrepreneur $500 to rent one of his vacant buildings for a week. Alton hadn't planned not to turn over the SS 100 X to James Spivey when he'd rented the space. He'd only thought it safer to plan the delivery by his own time schedule. He didn't like the idea of driving it into the caves without first getting his second $100,000 in hand.

Now, he worried that he might be in grave trouble if Jack Soo discovered he'd stolen the car and Alton didn't accept what Soo's business associates would certainly consider a reasonable offer. He also wondered just what in the hell was rolling around in the trunk.

Alton steered the Lincoln into the narrow alleyway behind Meza's storefront empire. He shoved a twelve-foot wooden garage door sideways on a rusty rail. There were four small windows in the door with glass so grimy they didn't need to be painted or boarded over to keep someone from looking in.

The concrete floor was cracked and oil spotted. A large puddle of fetid water occupied the middle of the dark room. The roof obviously leaked. Old plywood shelves lined one wall, the sort of shelves you threw up in the basement to hold half-empty cans of paint. Alton stepped around a broken dresser lying on its back to flip a gritty light switch mounted to the near side of the door. Nothing happened.

Back in the car, Alton managed a sharp three-point turn in the alley and drove the SS 100 X into the dim building. Leaving the garage door open for light, he unlatched and raised the hood to disable the engine. The hood itself weighed a hundred pounds.

The engine was as clean as a new-car showroom model's. It was also huge. Alton eventually located the rotor cable and tugged it free from both ends. He let the hood fall back into place with an echoing bang. It fit nicely.

"That ain't no van," someone called from the doorway.

Alton recognized the voice. Without turning around, he worked the cable into the top of his khaki slacks. Alton pulled off his Royals cap and began peeling the latex gloves from his hands.

"Hey, Rooster, that you?"

"Yeah, it's me." He turned and walked toward the stocky figure in the doorway. "I didn't know you'd be up this early."

"I thought you said a van." Meza showed his teeth in what might have been taken for a grin. Alton was distracted. When he'd let the hood fall, he'd thought he heard something move in the trunk.

"It's a car instead," Alton deadpanned, stepping out into the alley. He wadded the gloves into the blue ballcap and closed the cap over them by creasing the bill together in his right hand.

"It's a goddam limousine. You're lucky it fit."

"Well, it did."

"Must be hot, huh?" Meza rubbed his goateed chin, still staring into the dark recesses of the building.

"Help me close the door," Alton suggested.

"I don't know, Rooster. I might have to charge you more for a limousine." Meza leaned back against the doorjamb, facing Alton. He crossed one meaty arm over the other, showing off the tattoo on the back of his hand. It was a red star in a black triangle, the official mark of the Wizards.

Alton wasn't going to make an offer. Whatever he said, Meza would want more. So he waited while the motorcyclist went into his act.

"Hey, you know me, Rooster. I'd give you my hat, man. But a limousine . . ."

"There are no lights, Meza."

"Yeah, there's no gas and no water, too. What you expect for five hundred, mirrors on the ceiling and a waterbed? Hey, what's on those little flags?"

"I don't know. The guy must own a yacht."

"I bet a guy that owns a yacht would get real upset you stole his limousine. You can't drive it, you know. Too easy to spot. It would be real easy to get caught."

"Did you see anyone following me?" Alton was trying not to get angry. He wanted Meza happy with their deal but he didn't want the man to think the Lincoln was all that valuable.

"No. But when you pull it out of there, I could get in big trouble, Rooster." Meza made a face to show he was thinking over the size of the trouble he could find himself in. "What're you getting anyway, ten grand?"

"Five," Alton said. "Five thousand and that's top dollar on these things."

"I suppose so," Meza said, still thinking it over. "I'll go 20 percent."

"Okay, I'll give you another five hundred. If you help me with this door, I'll give you another five."

"Up front."

"Up front," Alton agreed.

They managed to slide the old wooden door closed and Alton worked the iron hasp into place. He pulled a heavy padlock from his right pocket.

"Hey, Rooster, what's that for?"

Meza was right. A good kick would take the door down. A pair of bolt cutters would also do the trick. Still, he worked the lock through the staple and shoved it closed.

"It'll keep out the curious grade-schoolers."

"You don't need no lock," Meza said loudly. "Ain't nobody messes with me, Rooster. Nobody's going to bother your limousine."

He paid Meza from his wallet, then unbuttoned his long-sleeved khaki shirt. He picked up the ballcap from the alley and wrapped the khaki shirt around it. Alton wore a plain black T-shirt underneath.

"You come and go as you please," Meza said, accepting the bundle of shirt, cap and gloves from Alton. "Ain't nobody going to be bothering you, Rooster." Meza walked him to the end of the alley.

"Who you know would want to ride around in that thing anyway? John Wayne?"

Somewhat exhilarated, Alton caught the Thirty-ninth

Street bus east, picking up a Plaza transfer slip. He'd stolen countless automobiles during his career as a car thief, but this was the first time he'd set off a bomb. The power of the explosion had taken him by surprise and he hoped he never had cause to set off another one.

He pushed against the socket of his right eye with the back of his hand. The eye burned unceasingly from the dose of gunpowder he'd carelessly rubbed into it. Out on Fifty-fifth Street, the local news crews videotaped his handiwork. Alton went back over everything he'd done. It hadn't been a perfect crime, but it was a good one. Forrest Jennings couldn't even tell anyone the car had been stolen.

Alton changed out of his work clothes in his van. He'd ditch the pants and shoes. He'd also throw away his socks. It wasn't likely he'd be caught, but he couldn't afford to have microscopic traces of gunpowder found on his clothes. Struggling to keep from rubbing his swelling eye, he walked into the Alameda to make a phone call.

Using a public pay phone, Alton dialed one of the two numbers he was supposed to call once he'd stolen the car. James Spivey answered his direct line.

Alton said, "Mission accomplished."

"Who is this?" the young attorney asked. "Franklin, is that you?"

"Yup."

"Okay, okay," Spivey rushed, thinking. "Look, I'm still at home. I have the phone coded . . . Give me thirty minutes, then bring it to the caves. Let's see . . . Yeah, thirty minutes will give me time to get the money together and get there ahead of you. Dock 38, remember?"

"Screw that," Alton said flatly.

"Listen, Franklin, we had a deal. You were supposed to let me know ahead of time."

"I have a better idea. Just calm down and listen."

"Dammit, Franklin, don't mess with me."

"Likewise," Alton said, not about to lose his temper. "If you think I'm driving a $13 million car into an underground warehouse where someone's waiting for me, you're nuts. I'm not touching that car again. Now, you either pay me and I give you the key and tell you where you can pick it up, or I go elsewhere."

"Elsewhere?"

"I've had other offers, asshole. I'm doing you a favor."

"Who? You wouldn't dare."

"Jack Soo, if you must know. He offered me the kind of money people change identities and move to foreign countries for."

"He offered you the kind of money people *die* for, Franklin. We know you're not going to talk. But Soo doesn't. He's not going to pay you, he's going to kill you."

"I thought of that," Alton admitted. "All I want is my money and to get my butt out of town."

"I don't like it. We can wait until night if you don't want to drive the thing around in broad daylight. But we have a deal and you're supposed to deliver."

"Tough shit."

Alton waited through a long pause while the attorney thought things over.

"You want more money? I don't think it's possible . . ."

"Of course it's possible," Alton said. "But I only want what was promised me. You meet me at Twin City Tavern at noon. You know where that is?"

"That grease-burger bar at State Line and Westport Road?"

"It'll be crowded then. You bring the money and I give you the key and tell you where the car is."

"Dammit, if somebody followed you, they could be stealing it out from under your nose right now. It's been on the news already, the blast. They got the pickup and I'm nervous about it, Franklin."

"Take it easy. You didn't buy the truck yourself?"

There was no reply.

"Spivey? Tell me you didn't buy the truck yourself."

"I did what you said. I got it through the want ads and paid cash. I even wore a disguise."

Alton laughed. "A red wig, no doubt. And falsies."

"It's not funny, Franklin. They have a witness who saw the car leaving Jennings' house right after the explosion. Some Good Samaritan. But he thought it came out of the carriage house and he said it was a brand-new limo, black."

"Good enough, let them go around looking for that."

"You don't understand. I'm in this up to my eyeballs. If anything goes wrong, I . . ."

"That's what you're paid for. Nothing's going wrong, so quit worrying. The car's safe. You're safe. Jennings won't say a word. Chances are he's pointing the cops in the opposite direction."

"I don't know, I don't know," Spivey stammered.

"Maybe you weren't cut out for a life of crime, counselor. Give that some thought the next time your client wants you to have something stolen for him. Twin City at noon." With that, Alton hung up.

Walking toward the elevators, it hit him. The flashbacks of the television coverage. Jack Kennedy's hand going up. Jackie's pink outfit as she clambered onto the back of the SS 100 X. A policeman's motorcycle in the grass. Alton knew then what was in the trunk. He cursed his luck.

CHAPTER NINE

Alton parked his van at a laundromat on Thirty-ninth Street. Marilyn Monroe appearing suddenly on the sidewalk in front of him, her pleated skirt blown up above her waist, wouldn't have slowed his determined march along the several sunlit blocks to Meza's row of dingy buildings. Alton wore a dark brown windbreaker zipped up, a flashlight in one pocket, a small set of picks and something that looked like a rechargeable electric screwdriver in the other. In 1961, American cars were manufactured with a separate trunk lock that required its own key.

He slid open the bulky door only far enough to slip inside, then closed it behind him. Enough daylight crept into the building that he'd only need the flashlight to pick the trunk lock. Alton opened the front passenger door of the Lincoln and plopped down in the seat to check the glove compartment for a key to the trunk.

Inside were a Secret Service radio code book and a black leather wallet. Twenty-six dollars in bills were folded into the wallet that also held a Commonwealth of Massachusetts driving license.

License 05332D was the only identification in the wallet. Alton turned on the flashlight to study it more closely. The signature may as well have been in Latin. It was entirely illegible. But the typed-in text identified the license as being issued to one John F. Kennedy, residing at 122 Bowden Street, Boston.

His stats were similar to Alton's: height 6/00, hair code 4 (brown), eye code 6 (gray). Only the color of Alton's eyes varied on his own driver's license. His were brown. The small card listed JFK as weighing only five pounds more than Alton.

The date of birth of the President was listed as 05/29/17. To Alton Franklin, 1917 was ancient history. John Kennedy, on the other hand, was perpetually young. He hadn't aged a day in more than a quarter century.

A chill played up and down his spine as he thought of that day in Dallas in 1963. The license expired May 29, 1965.

There was no spare key in the glove compartment. Neither could he find one under the front seat. Alton slipped the wallet into his empty back pocket and carried the flashlight to the rear bumper of the twenty-one foot Lincoln. He set the flashlight and automatic lockpick on the chrome step to the right of the spare-tire housing.

The battery-operated pick was true state-of-the-art and would open any auto lock, including GM's recent sidebar design, as well as most government and high-security locks. The pick worked off a spinning cam roller and, for noise reduction, two Teflon bearings. With the correct diamond-notched blade inserted, the device would open a common door lock in three seconds. Or less.

Auto locks took a bit longer. But first, you had to find the lock. Alton couldn't locate it. It was to neither side of the recessed spare-tire cover. It wasn't under or above it.

Alton cocked his head slightly sideways and closed his itching right eye, staring stupidly at the blue-on-white District of Columbia license plate GG 300.

He was considering buying a crowbar from a nearby hardware store when the fog lifted and he remembered something in the Ford Motor Company news release. The customized Lincoln Continental had an automatic trunk lid. And all power accessories were controlled by the driver, using individual switches on the dashboard console unit.

Up front in the driver's seat, Alton played with the switches, the ignition key turned to "on" position. He turned on, then quickly off, a nonglare floodlight that illuminated the backseat, the flashing red fireball lights inside the front grillwork, and a siren. The half-whoop of the siren echoed inside the dim building and he feared Meza would come running.

Alton caught his breath and tried to relax. He could be wrong, after all, about what had been rolling around in the trunk. He'd only come to allay his fears, he told himself, before turning over the SS 100 X.

The next switch he tried created a whirring noise but with no visible result. Another switch operated the sliding-glass partition between the driver's seat and the rest of the limo. If only there'd been an owner's manual in the glove compartment, he could have looked this thing up. Still another switch turned on two small spotlights that illuminated the flagstaffs on each front fender. Now, that was handy.

To his relief, Alton finally flipped the switch that popped open the trunk. About time, he thought, afraid he'd accidentally call in a nuclear strike on Cuba if he pushed any further switches.

Climbing out of the front seat, he tripped, his shoe catching on one of the power-operated metal steps extended from under the Lincoln. Why hadn't the Secret Service used those during the Dallas motorcade? He wondered, for that matter, why there hadn't been anyone riding the rear-bumper footholds and trunk-lid handgrips.

Alton wasn't prepared for what he saw in the carpeted trunk. There were two bodies, instead of one. And she was on top.

Miss Buddery was still in white, but wearing much less of it than the night before. A pair of panties to be precise.

They shone in the beam of his flashlight, as did her milk-white breasts.

Her body had that heavy-sleep appearance of the recently dead, her arms resting at odd angles where the weight of their flesh had taken them. Hers was a body at the mercy of gravity. Behind her, the body of Forrest Jennings appeared crammed into place, broken, stacked. His mouth was open and dry, his tongue swollen. A silk maroon robe was bunched above his waist, stained with blood as black as ink where it had soaked into the dark fabric.

Alton gulped, breathed deeply, then leaned slightly forward for a closer look. Her breasts were rising and falling, but ever so slightly. He reached a hand into the open trunk and placed it against her parted lips, feeling the moisture of her mouth on his palm, touching the faint tickle of her breath. She wore her emerald and diamond earrings. He didn't know if she'd been clubbed, drugged or shot. She could have been breathing poison gas from the exhaust system of the limousine for that matter.

Someone had to save her. And he was the only man in the room.

Setting aside the flashlight, he stepped against the bumper and, leaning in, worked his hands under her pliant flesh. He lifted her torso forward, pulling her body into a fold inside his arms. She moaned. If this were Sleeping Beauty, she couldn't have been prettier. Or heavier.

Only anorexic women weigh less than a sack of Portland cement. The woman in white was no exception. Alton cradled her against his straining chest and heaved upward, hoping his back stood the test. With a grunt, he erected himself and stepped back from the trunk to catch his balance.

Miss Buddery's arm, as if in a trance, went automatically around Alton's neck, her nearer breast flattening against him, impressing the tender flesh with the cold metal of his windbreaker's open zipper strip. Quickly, he let her feet drop, but she wouldn't stand up.

Her long legs dangled and he had to wrap both arms around her hips to hold her up. Her face rested into his shoulder, smudging the brown cloth with the residue of her makeup and her scent. The woman was dying, he thought. This wasn't the time for dancing cheek to cheek. Shuffling his shoes on the concrete floor, Alton walked backward around the side of the SS 100 X, the full weight of her body pressed into him.

She was warm and alive, but barely. Forrest Jennings, on the other hand, was as dead as a can of tuna and Alton worried about that in an immediate way.

She sat slumped in the front seat of the dark blue limo, holding her head in both hands to immobilize it, when Alton returned from the used-clothing boutique at end of the row of Meza's sagging buildings. He'd asked the girl there to call Meza and ask him to come around, alone.

Alton's living beauty wore his unzipped windbreaker over her shoulders. He stood inside the propped-open passenger door and held out an upturned palm to her.

"Here."

"What is it?" she asked, without moving her head, without opening her eyes.

"Aspirin. And a diet Pepsi. Take these and I'll open the can."

"I can't," she complained in a soft voice. "I can't move my head. It's all screams inside."

"You were drugged. The bruises on your leg and your back are from when they loaded you into the trunk. Now, take these."

Slowly, she removed a hand from the side of her face and stretched it weakly out toward him. Hers was a face that was everything Alton liked in faces, with one or two improvements he'd never dreamed of. He placed the four white tablets in the cup of her palm. He wanted to watch her green eyes flutter open, but she kept them tightly shut.

"Thanks, but I can't swallow these."

Alton popped the top on the can of diet soda.

"Sure you can. Just don't throw your head back to do it."

She carefully ate the aspirin from her hand as if it were popcorn she held to her mouth. When she refused the soda, with a cautious wave of her hand, Alton stepped back.

"How can you do that without something to drink?"

"I can't," she repeated.

"I brought you some clothes," Alton offered. "A pair of jeans, size ten. A T-shirt and tennis shoes. The shoes might be too big for you but I figured that was better than too tight."

"You're quite the gentlemen. Do I have to stand up? I think I'll throw up if I do . . ." Instead of trying to stand up in the open door of the car, she leaned forward by inches until her elbows were on her knees. "Take your jacket."

"Don't mind if I do. I've never been one to discourage a young woman from taking off her clothes."

"Don't bet on it. Hand me that shirt. I'll start with that." She accepted the T-shirt loosely in one hand and then fell over sideways in slow-motion with a groan, clutching the cotton shirt to her chest. Meza rattled the sliding door to the building and Alton hurried to intercept him there. He did his best to explain what he needed without telling Meza too much.

"I don't like it," the motorcyclist said. "You think I got a freezer here for putting a body in?"

"I've got an idea about that," Alton countered.

"Why don't you just dump it somewhere? I could help you with that."

"I don't know who killed him," Alton said as he considered the offer.

"And you're going to find out," Meza charged sarcastically.

Alton sighed, stalling.

"I have to know who it is if you want me to help."

"Forrest Jennings."

"The rich guy? His house was blown up today. Saw it on the TV. Hey, Rooster, you did that, didn't you? Damn, man—you did that!"

"But I didn't kill him. He was in the trunk of the car."

"Well, if you didn't kill him, whoever did is going to kill you. You drove off with the body. They're going to be looking for it. And when they find it, they'll kill you and then they'll kill me. I don't like it."

"That's why I'm paying you."

"Screw that. It'll cost you, but I ain't doing this for money. Hell, they find out the body was here and it's my ass. You know as well as me who goes around shooting people and putting their bodies in trunks and it sure as hell ain't the Junior League."

Alton waited for Meza to get it off his chest. The motorcyclist couldn't turn him away now and he couldn't turn Alton in.

"Damn," Meza went on, "you rent somebody a place to park a car and they start bringing around bodies the mob has shot up. What's this country coming to?"

"You'll help then?"

"Yeah, okay. But, I get the plunder on top the fee."

"Not the car," Alton emphasized.

"Who'd want it? It looks like a convertible hearse in the first place, and now you got this dead rich guy tied to it. I tell you, Rooster, I'd burn the damn thing if I was you."

Meza left. Alton waited impatiently for his return.

When the biker came back he was carrying a rolled sleeping bag, as Alton had suggested. Alton closed the sliding door behind him and led Meza through the dimness toward the rear of the SS 100 X, its trunk lid up.

"Who's the babe?" Meza asked, pausing to give her an interested once-over. The woman lay on her back in the front seat, one hand loosely holding the T-shirt to her chest, the other covering her forehead and both eyes.

"Sleeping Beauty," Alton said. "Come on back here with that."

Meza unrolled and zippered open the sleeping bag on the concrete floor behind the trunk. Jennings had been shot twice in the chest, Alton discovered as they lifted his stained and stiffening body from the trunk. Once the body was stretched out on the sleeping bag, Meza adjusted Jennings' silk robe to cover the dead man's genitals. Then he went to work.

The woman in white stirred feebly in the front seat, sitting up and tugging on the T-shirt over her throbbing head. She walked faintly toward the rear of the car, clutching the side of the SS 100 X with each step, in time to see Meza forcing a large ring off Jennings' right hand. It was platinum with matching rubies to either side of a polished lapis-lazuli stone.

"Must have been his father's," Meza said, pocketing it. "It was a little big for him." He also removed a very expensive gold watch with a gold, diamond-studded watchband. From around Jennings' swelling neck Meza unclasped a heavy gold chain. It looked to weigh about two pounds, Alton thought.

Miss Buddery leaned forward suddenly and threw up, gagging on her empty stomach.

"She's the sensitive kind," Alton explained.

"Never die with your jewelry on, sweetie," Meza said to her, laughing hoarsely.

The corpse's flesh was bluish gray, the color of an uncooked sausage sleeve. Last night, Alton thought, he'd been a powerful, boastful man. Today he was just another piece of raw meat. One way or the other, it happened to everybody. Even presidents, he recalled, closing the lid of the trunk quietly, as you close the cover of a book once you've come to the end.

CHAPTER TEN

Miss Buddery lay on the bed in her loose jeans and wrin-
kled T-shirt, a damp washrag over her head. Occasion-
ally, she would moan almost inaudibly or try to sit up as a
thought struck her and fall back on the bed to moan
more loudly. Alton had flushed his right eye with cold
water from the lavatory sink. He was on the phone, his
back to her, letting it ring a dozen times, just in case
Monique was in the shower or still asleep. She never
woke up easily.

Eventually, a man answered with a quiet but uneasy
"Hello?"

Alton asked for Mike, not wanting to alarm whoever it
was in his and Monique's room across the hall at the
Alameda. He belligerently confirmed the room number
with feigned impatience, then hung up on whoever the
hell it was loitering in the room.

He could discern from the brief words they'd ex-
changed that it wasn't James Spivey. And neither was it
Jack Soo, but it might have been one of Soo's associates.
Alton was filled with the worst kind of fear for Monique.
He had to find her.

Alton dialed the room again, letting it ring only once
before hanging up. And again, wanting whoever was in
there to come out. He called one more time for the hell
of it and bounded to the door of the hotel room he'd
taken under an assumed name the day he and Monique
had checked into the Alameda. His eye to the peephole,
he could easily see the door of the room across the hall.

"Come on," he whispered encouragement. "Come on, you bastard. You'd better get out of there."

Not as surprised as he should have been, Alton watched Rick Feigen step quickly out the opening door, look both ways with a cautious grin on his face, then stroll casually away as the door closed behind him. If Jack Soo could figure out where they were staying, why not the white-haired gentleman?

Everyone else at the auction knew by now that the Jennings mansion had been bombed and had a good idea, no doubt, that the SS 100 X had been stolen. Alton wondered how many people knew that Forrest Jennings was dead. Somebody else knew. That was for sure. Was it Feigen?

Alton counted to ten, slowly, then stepped out into the hall, room key in hand. Inside the room, he discovered that Monique wasn't there. Perhaps she'd been taken hostage. The bed was unmade and her clothes were in piles about the room. But that was normal for Monique. Her purse was gone, which he took as a good sign. The odds against her having been abducted shifted slightly. Alton called it even money and checked out the bathroom.

There were two damp Alameda towels puddled on the floor, signs Monique had taken a shower. A pair of uneaten gherkins floated in the toilet. He flushed the toilet, watching the pickles dance atop the churning water. They refused to be flushed.

He'd done a good job of getting away with the car. But he couldn't feel right about it. He'd also stolen a nifty little murder out from under someone. His own small bag of toiletries remained unmolested in the top drawer of the dresser. Alton grabbed it and the Jack Soo bottle of scotch.

Exiting, he dangled from the doorknob the sign that said "Do Not Disturb" in seven different languages. He hoped Monique got the message, should she return.

"It's an anesthetic," Alton insisted, handing Miss Buddery a finger of golden liquor he'd poured into a hotel glass. Her eyes slitted against the light, she sipped at the scotch without moving her head. Alton took the glass from her and set it on the bedside table. From his bag, he removed four tablets of a non-aspirin pain reliever and a single Robin Egg. The blue-spotted pill was a mild hit of the speed that Alton kept on hand for the long solitary drives between racing meets and seasons. He needed her roused and he didn't have all day to wait.

Alton took up her hand and placed the pills in it. "Take these." He handed her the glass he'd filled with water.

Calling room service, he watched her in the dresser mirror to make certain she took her medicine. Alton ordered up two complete breakfasts and two pots of coffee.

"What's your name?" he asked, sitting on the edge of the bed, nearest her feet.

"Isabel Buddery. But I go by Liz."

"Frankie," Alton said without a hitch. "Very nice to make your acquaintance."

"I know who you are." Liz lay back down and replaced the washrag to her forehead.

"Just trying to be polite."

"Oh God," she moaned heavily. "This is not a date. You can cut the country charm."

"Who killed him?"

"I won't be able to eat."

"Sure you will," Alton said cheerfully. "And then we've got work to do."

"We?"

"I'm afraid your ass isn't worth betting on right now. Someone's very upset that you're still alive. They didn't stick you in that trunk for a joyride, darling."

"Don't call me darling."

"Isabel Buddery," Alton mused aloud. "English?"

"Quite."

The agitation, he figured, would do her good. Of course the speed wouldn't hurt.

"What part?" Alton asked, keeping it going.

"Waist up. I have strong teeth." Alton laughed. Now they were getting somewhere. "My ass, as you so demurely expressed it, was raised in the States. Manhattan, to be exact."

"Who killed him, Liz?"

"I don't know."

"Whoever killed him drugged you. My guess is some kind of veterinarian tranquilizer. Bimbos use it to knock out tricks they're going to rob."

"Did you say *bimbos?*"

"Well, they aren't girls you'd want to fall in love with."

"I don't doubt that."

"Did you see anything?"

"No."

"What's the last thing you remember?"

"You asking *me* if I saw anything," she said bitterly.

Alton considered forcing her head into the toilet bowl and flushing it until she was ready to cooperate. But, even recovering from a tranquilizer overdose and draped in somebody else's crummy clothes, Liz Buddery didn't look like the sort of woman you'd do that to. She looked instead like the sort of woman, even though you knew she'd turn you down, you wanted to ask to dance.

"I'm on your side, Liz. If I wasn't, you wouldn't be alive right now. Try to remember that. We'll talk after breakfast."

"I won't be able to eat," she reiterated.

But Liz did eat, nibbling weakly at small bits of Canadian bacon and at the corners of her toast, her scrambled eggs left entirely untouched. After her third cup of coffee, Liz Buddery's green eyes seemed to regain their light.

"How long have you been in Kansas City?" Alton placed his silverware on his empty plate.

"A couple of years. Give or take an eternity."

Then out of the blue she cursed, throwing her hands to her ears.

"What is it?"

"My earrings. Dammit, they're gone!"

"You'd better give up on those," Alton advised. "It's not a good idea right now to go back to Jennings' place and ask for your stuff."

"I had them on."

"You go to bed with your jewelry on?"

"In this case," Liz said. "That Mexican biker took them. I've got to get them back. They're very . . . important to me." Alton knew she'd started to say that they were very valuable, very expensive. *Important* was a nice way of putting it.

"I don't think so," Alton said. "But I'll ask him about it."

"He robbed a corpse, didn't he?"

"But he asked permission first. It was part of the deal."

"Oh God, what are you people?"

"Thieves and whores. And you?"

Liz didn't reply.

"A slut in a fur coat is supposed to be something special where you come from?" Alton had had enough. "You're some kind of golden girl, is that it? Who wears diamonds and emeralds when she beds rich men? Tell me this, Liz, does their semen taste like silver when you're swallowing it?"

She turned away, reddening with indignation.

"I'll tell you what, I've been to New York. I've been to Manhattan, Liz. And the women I met there could have used a douche once they climbed down from their high horse." Alton seethed.

"Is that asinine analogy supposed to contain meaning?" she said, standing from the table too quickly, having to grasp the back of her chair to regain her impaired equilibrium.

"I'm angry!" Alton shouted.

"You're stupid," she retaliated. "You're stupid and insulting."

"And the only friend you've got right now. The only person who can keep you alive."

"Why, pray tell, would you want to?" Isabel Buddery sank back to the bed. Alton paced off his remaining rage, forcing himself to think. Glancing at his watch, he saw that he was behind schedule.

"It's eleven-thirty. I've got to meet somebody at noon . . ." Alton's voice trailed off, realizing as he said it that he'd be standing up James Spivey today. The kid lawyer would just have to wait.

Alton sat back down on the bed. Liz lay on her face. He wanted to put his hand on her leg, the small of her back. Touching her would dispel his anger completely. Alton had met a young black man from South Africa in prison. Davis Makande had told Alton that if he touched somebody on the shoulder when they were arguing, the anger would go away. It was a common practice among the tribesmen, a method of healing ill will.

He wanted to try it out on Liz. Instead, he let his mind spin. Alton rose from the bed and checked through the peephole to see if anything was going on across the hall. The "Do Not Disturb" sign was still in place.

"I've got it." He crossed back into the room. "The bald guy. He did it. That duel was a ruse, an alibi of sorts."

"I don't think so." Liz rolled over on the bed. She wasn't smiling; she stared vacantly into some inner middle ground. "Harold Muleford liked torturing him. They fought each other constantly."

"Screw that macho crap," Alton said. "He wanted the car."

"Everybody wanted the car," Liz said.

"Speaking of which, who is Rick Feigen? You know, the white-haired guy?"

"According to Jennings, he's CIA."

"CIA?"

"He was representing the government's interest at the auction. Jennings didn't want them to have it. He was afraid they would destroy the car. It would be a major embarrassment if Kennedy's death car was found to exist."

"But the government owns it in the first place," Alton said.

"Not really. The SS 100 X was leased by Ford Motor Company to the White House at $500 a year. After the assassination, Ford allowed the car to be absorbed, but they still own it."

"Whether they ever claim it or not."

"Since Ford went along with the cover-up, they probably wouldn't care to press the issue," Liz informed him, her green eyes focusing. "The CIA just wants to keep the car from coming to light. If Feigen got his hands on the car, I'm sure they would destroy it."

"Cover-up?" Alton asked. "What do you mean?"

"The official line was that the SS 100 X was remade into President Johnson's limo. New upholstery, added steel, eight-paned bulletproof glass, the works. But J. Edgar Hoover wanted to keep it available for evidence. It was going to be years before the investigations were over. And, as you know, the Warren Commission settled nothing."

"So the FBI had the car."

"So it was assumed. When Hoover died, the car was missing. The CIA began the search. Nobody knows for certain how long the car's been in private hands. But Jennings' foolhardy little auction was as close as they've come to getting it back."

"Would Feigen kill Jennings to get the car?"

Liz thought it over. "Too risky. If the car was sold, it had to be moved. Feigen was probably devising ways to get control of it then." She paused. "By the way, how did you get the car out of the house?"

"By the way," Alton countered, "just who do you represent? The Lollipop Guild?"

CHAPTER ELEVEN

Sleeping Beauty turned out to be a bear. But, after some serious face twisting, she seemed to come clean. Alton liked to believe that she feared for her life and needed him to keep her safe. Yet it could have been because he had control of the Lincoln Continental that she buttered him up. Perhaps Alton was being greased for the frying pan.

"Harold Muleford," she said, glancing away.

"Oh, that's lovely." Alton laughed, but there was no humor in it.

"Everybody works for somebody. I could be asking you the same question."

"And you'd get an honest answer."

"Give me a break," Liz protested. "I'm telling the truth."

"All right then, fill me in."

"He hired me to get along with Jennings, for the same reason you brought Miss Orange Polka-dots to the auction, I presume."

"At least that would explain why you were drugged instead of killed," Alton said, ignoring the insult. "And now that the body and the car are missing, I doubt Muleford will be so generous next time. You're walking testimony that a murder took place. Hell, he's looking for you right now."

"He's looking for the car," Liz corrected. "Everyone is."

"So tell me about Harold Muleford."

"What's there to tell? He's been pulling stunts like that

duel for years. He and Forrest Jennings were crosstown rivals. They went to the same high school and that's all they have in common. Jennings was popular, rich, top of the class. He was first-string in everything and Muleford sat the bench. Jennings was born to affluence. Muleford created his own."

"I know. Jack Rabbit Transit. They're Hopping to Please. I've seen the trucks."

"Jennings was tall, suave and good-looking. Muleford was a pudge," she continued. "He got a job driving trucks out of high school, while Jennings took a degree in liberal arts at Princeton."

"I get the picture."

"And the ketchup? Did you know about the ketchup?"

Alton let her tell it. The speed was kicking in. Isabel Buddery's green eyes danced from thought to thought as she talked.

"When Jennings started Au Natural ice cream, Muleford came up with this specialty ketchup. It was supposed to be a gourmet ketchup. He dropped lots of money on it and it came up a dud. He blames Jennings for it failing, naturally, and he's still trying to get even."

"Gourmet ketchup?"

"Nobody ever went broke underestimating the taste of the American public," Liz quoted. "It's been back and forth between them ever since. Muleford had agents outbid Jennings at every art auction in the Midwest. Jennings loved fine art. Muleford loved besting Jennings.

"You couldn't go to an art auction in Chicago without seeing both of them there. Muleford would sit and stare at Jennings, while his bidding agents took up the price on everything Forrest attempted to buy. In the end, Jennings bid on the worst things just to get Muleford to pay exorbitant prices for real pieces of crap. Eventually, Muleford caught on and that was the conclusion of that little war."

Alton poured himself a sliver of Johnnie Walker. It was

noon. He swirled the liquid in his glass and inhaled the scent. Given time, you could get drunk smelling scotch.

"The whole thing escalated. Jennings was the bon vivant bachelor his entire life. And he slipped in the side door and bedded Muleford's wife."

Alton arched his eyebrows, sipping.

"It probably wasn't all that difficult," Liz said. "But he let Muleford know about it. He was supposed to have taken pictures of himself and Mrs. Muleford in bed."

"Nice guy," Alton said.

"It was just one more thing, you see. There were plenty of battles between them."

Alton recalled the vile look in Muleford's eye when he'd fired the dum-dum into Forrest Jennings' diamond-studded chest. Muleford's expression had been forged from years of loathing. His face was that of a murderer's.

"Divorce?" Alton asked.

"Definitely," Liz said. "She was probably waiting for an opportunity to ditch Muleford all along. You can bet she received a healthy settlement. Not all dealings in the trucking business are up-and-up. She knew a few things, had accompanied him on trips to the Cayman Islands and the like."

"Ah, yes, our hemisphere's Mecca of banking outside the dominion of the IRS." Given Jack Soo's $2 million, Alton would pay a visit to the Cayman Islands himself. He carried his drink to the peephole and surveyed the hallway.

"Where does the car come in?" Alton asked, coming back to lean against the dresser.

"That was another victory for Jennings."

"In the beginning," Alton corrected her. "When you're dead and the other guy's alive you can't really say that you won."

"Muleford loves cars. He owns a few classics he keeps warehoused here in town. Muleford found himself on the A-list of people allowed to bid on the SS 100 X. It was being sold someplace near Cleveland. The funny thing is that Muleford was contacted because of his regular appearances at art auctions in the region. Anyway, nothing was going to keep Muleford from owning that car. He would have sold off Jack Rabbit Transit if that's what it took."

"But Jennings beat him to the draw?"

"Somehow Jennings got in on it," she explained. "He bought the car before the auction by paying cash up front. To save face, the auction went on as planned. The bidders weren't allowed to see the car. No one knew where it was stored. And no one knew who'd won the bid. Muleford was terribly depressed when he learned he'd lost out. He couldn't believe his open-ended bid had been rejected after he'd been invited to participate."

Alton knew how he felt. He'd once been invited to apply for an American Express card and then had been turned down.

"Of course Jennings let him know he had the SS 100 X," Liz said. "That's about it."

"No, it's not." Alton again checked the peephole. All was empty in the circular realm of the hallway.

"What?"

"That's not about it, Liz. There's more. There's the part where Muleford drugs you, kills Jennings, puts you both in the trunk of the car and prepares to drive happily away with his conquest."

"How?" she asked aloud, puzzling it out for herself.

"That's what I've been wondering. Maybe they were going to knock out the wall from the inside."

"No," Liz said. "I mean how did you get it out of the mansion?"

"I took down the wall from the outside. Trade secret."

"I see." She let it go at that.

Alton had hoped she'd be more impressed by his feat of derring-do. It hadn't been the charge up San Juan Hill, but it had taken a degree of reckless courage to steal that car.

Isabel Buddery had thoughts of her own. "There's just one small catch to your theory," she said. "Muleford didn't drug me. Forrest Jennings did."

There wasn't time for Alton to ask further questions. Faint sounds of a doorknob rattling captured his immediate attention. He shot to the peephole in time to see Monique go into the room across the hall.

"Be right back," he told Liz.

"What are you doing in her room? What is she doing here?" Monique loudly demanded to know. Her dark eyes flashed, instantly recognizing Isabel Buddery as the woman at the auction last night despite her disheveled appearance.

"Take it easy," Alton said in an attempt to soothe her ruffled female feathers. "Sit down and listen to me for a minute. It's important."

Alton considered just how much to tell Monique. For her own good he needed her to stay in the room when he and Liz left. Alton couldn't risk crossing paths with James Spivey. His van was a sitting duck in the Alameda parking garage.

Monique sat on the unoccupied bed and sulked.

"There's been a murder," Alton said, getting to the heart of it. "Our lives are at risk."

Monique looked up at him sternly, then stared with open hostility at Liz. "Are you two screwing?" she asked point-blank. " 'Cause if you're screwing, Frankie, I'm out of here. I'm leaving. You promised you were taking me to Louisville and . . ."

"I am taking you to Louisville," Alton said. "Just clam up and listen, will you? This is very serious business."

Monique pouted. She didn't like being told to shut up.

She certainly didn't like Alton staying in another hotel room with a woman he'd met the night before.

Alton sat on the edge of the bed, looking straight into Monique's questioning eyes. "Isabel here was attacked and Forrest Jennings was murdered. This time for real. I've seen the body."

"This has to do with that car, doesn't it?"

"What do you know about the car?" Alton asked, surprised.

"Lots," Monique taunted. "It's worth a lot of money, I know that. And it was stolen this morning, I know that. And you did it, Frankie. You stole the car. You stole it for money, and I don't give a shit—so let's go to Louisville."

"We will, we will," Alton said, thinking. "Who told you this?"

Monique remained petulantly silent. She didn't mind having the upper hand, if only for a moment.

"Who?" Alton nearly shouted.

"Rick," she said spritely. "The nice guy from last night."

"I know who Rick Feigen is," Alton barked.

Liz was wisely staying out of the conversation.

"Well, he thought I knew all about it, Frankie. He called this morning and woke me up, said he wanted to buy the car from us. I put two and two together after he told me it had been stolen earlier. I'm not as dumb as you think I am. You've been acting pretty squirrelly since we got here."

"What else?"

"He was going to come by. I thought you were going to sell it to that other guy and figured you'd be upset. But he knew the room number, Frankie. I thought you must have told him. I took a quick shower and got dressed, then . . ." She stopped, her memory catching a snag.

"Then what?"

"What are those pickles doing in the toilet?" Monique asked.

"Forget it," Alton said quickly. "I needed the jar."

"Then I got cold feet. I didn't know where you were and I thought I might have made a mistake. After that Oriental guy and all last night, I thought this car thing was too big to mess with. So I ran out and got breakfast. They have some really nice places over there." Monique gestured with her head, indicating the Country Club Plaza. "I looked at all the fountains," she added.

"Okay," Alton said. "You did the right thing."

"How long have you been here?" Monique asked, eyeing the dirty plates on the side table.

"Not very. Now, listen, people are looking for Isabel and me. And now they're looking for you. It's not just the car any longer. Whoever murdered Forrest Jennings probably wants us out of the way, too. We're the only ones who know he's been killed. And I've got something the murderer wants."

"The car? You did steal it, didn't you?"

"Forget about the car," Alton said. "If it was just the car, we'd leave town right now. It's much worse than that. I've got to find out who killed Jennings and get something on him. Otherwise, they'll follow us to Louisville. They'll chase me down wherever I go." The other half of his motivation was to protect Liz, but Alton figured Monique didn't want to hear that part.

"Is it really that bad, Frankie?"

"It really is. Monique, I'm sorry I got you into this. And I promise we'll go to Louisville as soon as this is all over. But you can't leave the room. That's imperative. A man I was supposed to meet at noon is going to come here in about half an hour. He's going to be very upset and I don't want you to get hurt."

"I'll wait till he leaves."

"No," Alton said. "There are others. There's Jack Soo from last night. His friends are looking for me, too."

"Are you going to get the money?"

"That's not important right now. It's just a car," Alton

said, believing it. "What I've got to do is confront the person who killed Forrest Jennings. It's the only way out of this mess."

"Do you have a gun, Frankie?"

He shook off her question. "Monique, just promise me you'll stay here until I get back. All right?"

"I guess so. Are you two leaving together?"

"It's nothing like that," Alton told her. "But you must stay here until you hear from me. Order food from room service, but don't tell them your name. Bill it to the room. Don't even step out into the hall when your food comes. It's vital that you don't leave this room."

"All right, already," she huffed. "I get the idea. But I tell you what, Frankie, this is the last time I ever date a gambler. You can bet on that."

Alton gripped her arm as he and Liz waltzed across the lobby.

"He's here," she said from the corner of her mouth.

"Who?"

"Rick Feigen," Liz told him. "Over there." She nodded.

Alton stopped and surveyed the massive lobby of the Alameda Plaza. There were people milling about everywhere. He squinted, closing his reddened eye.

"At the piano bar," she said.

"But it's not open yet."

"He's reading the newspaper."

"Of all the worn-out spook tricks," Alton muttered, taking her once more by the arm. His phone calls had scared Feigen off the room, but surely he'd noticed Monique coming through the lobby on her way to the elevators. It was just as certain that Mr. CIA was watching Liz and Alton exit the Alameda.

Isabel Buddery's skin felt warm under his fingertips, warm and alive. And her heat, Alton thought, was not the result of the amphetamine he'd given her.

CHAPTER TWELVE

"You could take me home," she said, climbing into the passenger seat of Alton's converted van.

"Not on your life." Alton showed Liz how to unlock and lock the swivel seat. "It looks to me as if whoever killed Jennings was at the house when I took the car. They must have been going to take down the wall. Maybe they'd already started. What time did you go to bed last night?"

"We don't need to go into that."

"Either way, Jennings was killed and you were put into that trunk alive. I came in and drove off with the both of you. You're as good as dead if the murderer finds you. And so am I once they figure out I have the car."

"That's probably been taken for granted by everyone at the auction. Jennings knew you were a car thief. Barnett did a little research after the invitations went out. Jennings just didn't give a damn. He didn't believe there was any way the car could be stolen."

"How did I get an invitation in the first place?"

"Someone with a lot of clout," Liz said. "Just like the rest of them. You didn't think Jennings believed you were bidding on the car for yourself?"

"No."

"You mean to tell me you didn't know who you were bidding for?" she asked, turning in her seat to face him. "That's a hoot."

"I figured Jennings knew," Alton shrugged. "I was hired by proxy."

"And you stole the thing without knowing who you were stealing for?"

"I guess so. The point is I have the car."

"Who's your contact?" Liz asked, suddenly interested.

"That's confidential."

"Nothing's confidential when you start coming into contact with people like Feigen. Jennings had everyone pegged. Jack Soo was fairly obvious. Forrest laughed about that. He kept asking me if I could imagine the SS 100 X in the front lobby of a Vegas casino behind velvet ropes. The trouble was that I could."

"And he knew Feigen was attempting to recover the car for the government?"

"Of course. And Jennings wished him luck. Once he sold it, he'd just as soon it went back underground. And, like I said, he honestly didn't believe anyone could take it from him."

"Who was the black guy?"

"David Cross," Liz answered primly.

"And who did he represent?"

"A Japanese holding company. What with the value of the yen these days, he could have outbid us all. You've seen what they've been paying for Van Goghs?"

"But Jennings wouldn't have been so un-American as to let the car go overseas?"

"True," she said. "In fact, I was the only one there who had any real chance of buying the car."

"How come? I mean, if Jennings had everyone pegged, how did he miss you? You were representing Muleford. He'd never have sold it to him. Not after that duel anyway."

Liz smiled slyly. "I had a front. A good one. Jennings fell for it."

"Muleford's better at this sort of thing than I thought. What was your front?"

"That's confidential," she said flatly.

"That leaves Feigen, Muleford and Jack Soo. Soo could

have done it, but I'm opting for Muleford. Jack Soo had other angles, just like Feigen. I think he was figuring to get the car once it was sold and had to be moved. And I think we can write off David Cross. The Japanese wouldn't have Jennings murdered like that. They wouldn't need to. He was probably the only one there who took the auction at face value."

"Probably," Liz said ambiguously.

"And Feigen's made us. He saw us together just now. If he killed Jennings and stuffed you in the trunk, he'd be right behind us."

"Maybe he is and we just can't see him."

"No. I've been watching that lobby door for a good ten minutes now. He's taking it easy, probably gone upstairs to bug my room."

Alton started the van and let it idle in park.

"Which reminds me," he said. "What did you mean when you said Forrest Jennings drugged you? He was dead. He was dead before you were stuffed into the car."

Isabel Buddery reddened, but the blush faded quickly from her cheeks. "I drank it. He slipped me a Mickey. I don't know what the hell he had in mind. I was in my room and we were, uh, we were getting ready to go to bed. He handed me a drink and I took a sip. It hit me like a hammer. I have no idea what he was up to."

"Were you dressed?"

"No," she said, her embarrassment passing. "I don't go to bed with my clothes on."

"But you wear your jewelry to beddy-bye?"

"Jennings asked me to. He's got this thing about jewels. He wanted to . . . well, he wanted me with my jewelry on."

"Then maybe *he* took your earrings." Alton backed the van from the parking slot. The squeal of his tires echoed off the concrete walls of the parking garage. He'd parked his van in full view of the lobby entrance through the garage entrance. There was no sense in sitting around waiting for James Spivey to show up.

Alton pulled the van into the warm sunlight of an April afternoon. He thought best when he was driving.

"What were you wearing at the time?" he asked.

"What do you mean? I told you I don't wear clothes to bed."

"Precisely what? It's important."

"Nothing really. My earrings."

"Were your panties on?"

"Yes," Liz replied, gazing distractedly out the passenger window at a car pulled alongside the van at a light. It was nobody she recognized.

"And what was Jennings wearing? When you passed out?"

"His robe, I think. Yes, he still had his robe on."

"Then he must have been killed soon after you slipped into unconsciousness. You still had your panties on when you were put into that trunk. And Jennings was still wearing his robe."

"Oh God," Liz moaned, the idea finally catching up to her. "You think he was a necrophiliac or something like that?"

"Something like that. Maybe he liked to take pictures and thought you wouldn't go along with it. Who knows?"

"But he didn't have to be killed right then. He might have been distracted. Say someone showed up and he went downstairs to deal with them. Hell, maybe he had a poker game scheduled. He could have been shot much later and they still would have found me passed out on the bedroom rug. And I don't believe for a minute that anyone but your biker friend took my earrings. Forrest Jennings wouldn't steal."

Alton laughed. "He'd drug his date, but he wouldn't steal. Sure. And besides, you're leaving someone else out —he may have your earrings."

"Who's that?"

"The murderer. It's been my experience that a man who kills can't be trusted not to walk off with the family silver. You've got to keep a proper reality, Liz."

She thought it over. "It's the biker," she insisted. "I just know he's got them."

Alton rubbed his eye. It didn't burn much at all any longer, but it felt horribly dry and itchy and it remained puffed.

"I've got an idea," he confessed, driving around the rear of the Nelson-Atkins Museum. "There's a hundred ways this thing might have happened. But that ploy of Muleford's was just too damn obvious. He hated Jennings. He wanted the car. Maybe he thought Jennings was on to you. So he came back, without the cops, and shot him. It may be simple, but it adds up. And, I'm telling you, there was murder in that man's eyes last night. You couldn't mistake that."

"So what do we do?"

"We get him to deal with us. We get to him and we get to him quickly. If he covers up, I'll be able to tell he's lying. I've heard a million lies and they all have one thing in common. They don't sound like the truth."

"We just drive over to his office, walk in the door, and ask him if he shot Forrest Jennings? And then you watch to see if his pupils dilate and we'll know if he did it?"

"Maybe. No, wait! Does his ex-wife still live in town?"

"Yes," Liz said. "But I'm not going over there in these filthy things."

"It doesn't matter. You're staying in the van. Where does she live?"

"Garden Meadows, off One-hundred-and-third. Listen, it won't hurt anything. We could run by Swansons or something. I can pick up something to wear and you can look her up in the phone book. I don't remember the house number. It's not like I've ever been invited to tea with Mrs. Muleford."

"I don't think so," Alton said. "You're staying in the van."

She looked at him and smiled slyly—her eyes coming on. "Frankie, you're so convinced my life is in immediate danger . . . well, I don't want to die in these rags. You can understand that, can't you?"

Clothes she wouldn't be caught dead in, Alton mused. He drove to the Kansas side.

Alton caught a direct look at Isabel Buddery's profile as he slowed for a light. Few women are truly beautiful from the side. Liz was clearly one of that select minority. Her mouth and chin were perfectly shaped. Her blazing green eyes shone from under naturally arched dark eyebrows. Hers was a gene pool William Shockley could dive into and never need come up for air.

Alton found Barbara Muleford's listing in the White Pages he borrowed at the service counter, while Liz shopped. She used the phone in the women's room, her primary purpose in suggesting the shopping trip, to call a man who didn't answer. Frustrated, she hung up. It was important she get in touch with him. She couldn't leave the SS 100 X just sitting there.

Liz showed admirable restraint, Alton thought, picking out a light blue sweater, black chinos and comfortable shoes. She drew closed the curtain behind the driver's seat and changed into her new clothes in the back of his van.

"Do you live in here or something?" she asked. Alton had pinned up the table and had folded down the bench seat into its bed, laying the back cushion down flat. It rode better that way.

"I'm seriously considering it," he called back to her.

"I think I need some more aspirin," Liz informed him as she climbed back into the passenger seat. Alton was surprised to see she held a small, new clutch purse in her lap.

"What's with the purse?" he wanted to know. "You don't have anything to put in it."

"Why, Frankie, don't you know that a woman never goes anywhere without a purse?"

It was the second time she'd called him by name. He could learn to like it.

"Besides," Liz added, "I've got to have something to put my earrings in when you get them back for me."

Garden Meadows turned out to be closer to One-hundred-and-fifteenth. It was another new subdivision of $400,000 homes with ten-cent fences around look-alike backyard swimming pools. Alton wasn't impressed. Only someone who didn't care where they lived, but perhaps only how they lived, would live in a place like this.

If he turned over the car to Jack Soo, Alton could buy himself a half-dozen of the three-story houses by the weekend. Or someone could buy for him a cemetery plot. Weighing outcomes of dealing with the Las Vegas mobster, Alton crossed Jack Soo's name off his "Things To Do" list.

He wanted to be a happy-go-lucky guy. Alton told himself if it hadn't been for the murder, he would be out of town by now. He and Monique would be on their merry way to Churchill Downs, one of them $200,000 richer. He wanted to be a happy-go-lucky guy, but gamblers rarely were.

Maybe it wasn't just the murder that kept him from turning over the car. His sticking around might have more to do with the woman riding next to him. Besides being drop-dead beautiful, Isabel Buddery was a gravely endangered species. Alton was convinced that without his help she would be dead soon. She was at that very moment being hunted by someone who damn well knew how to shoot. The American Wildlife Federation ought to push for a postage stamp of Isabel Buddery's likeness.

For one thing, she'd surely inspire more donations than any North American mountain goat.

First, he had to find out for certain who was behind the murder. Alton approached the puzzle as if it were a horse race. Muleford was the morning-line favorite for having shot his rival and stuffed him into the trunk of the SS 100 X. David Cross, according to Liz, wasn't in the running. That left Jack Soo, Rick Feigen and any outsider long shots Alton didn't know yet existed. He added Barnett, Jennings' butler-bodyguard, to the post parade just to round out the field.

To handicap Harold Muleford, Alton wanted a glance at the man's past performances, for which there is no better source than an ex-wife. Barbara Muleford, he hoped, would offer Alton the edge he required to approach the local king of trucking with the offer to make a deal that would ensure everybody's safety. But what would he ask Mrs. Muleford?

Parking on the spotless concrete street, Alton removed the keys from his van and pocketed them. Liz said she'd lie down in the back for a while. Barbara Muleford didn't answer the door. A tall, muscular blond with a protruding brow looked down at Alton and said, "Yeah?"

Obviously into his early forties, the man wore pink-soled white shoes, white cotton stirrup slacks and a white T-shirt. Alton noticed the man's large hands were shiny. He smelled of baby oil.

"Mrs. Muleford, please," Alton said in his strictly business voice. "I'm from Sargent Security."

"Yeah?" the big man repeated, showing lots of teeth without smiling.

"We're working on a major theft," Alton said. "I'd like to speak with Mrs. Muleford."

"Wait here." The man in the Jack LaLanne outfit closed the door in Alton's face. Alton tapped his toe. There wasn't much to see in the neighborhood. Every-

one's car was clean and expensive. Given a couple decades the skinny trees might grow into something worthy of a bird's nest. In the time it took to smoke a package
of cigarettes, Mr. Clean came back to the door to let him
in.

"This way," the monolith mumbled, putting two
words together to make a sentence for the second time
since they'd met. This guy would be great to down a few
beers with, Alton thought, if you were interested in being alone.

"Yeah?" Alton said lamely, stepping inside on a plush
smoky gray wall-to-wall carpet. Alton's eye itched. He
was led into a room done up in red Spanish tile and
steamed glass. A padded massage table looked recently
vacated, decked out in a crumpled white towel.

"You can leave now, Hans," a female voice instructed.
Hans slipped out the door into the backyard to have a
cigarette, no doubt, and to count the six or seven leaves
on the single-branch maple tree.

"If he shaved his head, he could have a career in com-
mercials," Alton told the woman, whose face floated in
the mist of a hot tub large enough to seat eight.

"I'm Mrs. Muleford. And you are?" The hot water
churned around her, adding a bubbly tenor to her voice.

"Robert Traver," Alton fibbed. "I'm a private detective working for Sargent Security. We've been employed
to investigate . . ."

"I'm sorry, dear, but I've never heard of you," she
interrupted. "Would you be so kind as to hand me a
towel? Unless of course you'd care to join me."

Alton snatched the towel from the massage table.
When he turned around, Barbara Muleford was already
climbing from the hot tub.

"I should have a robe somewhere," she said, walking
toward him, dripping. She looked good for her age, too
good. Alton suspected a tummy tuck and other surgical

adjustments had been performed on Mrs. Muleford's body. He handed her the towel, which Mrs. Muleford used to dry her hair.

"Don't be shy," she said.

CHAPTER THIRTEEN

Liz wasn't in the van when Alton returned.

Mrs. Muleford hadn't a thing to tell Alton, except that she and her ex-husband were still good friends. She agreed that if Forrest Jennings was missing something valuable Harold was a likely suspect. "They're out to get each other's goat," she'd said, "but they always take care of things like that between themselves."

Alton had asked if she believed Mr. Muleford capable of murdering Forrest Jennings. "My goodness no!" she'd insisted, then laughed. Alton couldn't help but notice the way her breasts jiggled when she laughed.

He started the engine, angry at himself for letting Isabel Buddery walk away so easily. There was a chance, if he hurried, Alton could catch her darting between the houses or across one of the streets. But Liz was smart enough to have knocked on somebody's door and to talk herself inside to use the telephone, he realized.

He'd have to look for her anyway. At the moment Alton put the van into gear, the passenger door jerked open and Liz hopped inside.

"Out for an April stroll?" Alton snapped, driving away from the curb with a squeal of tire biting concrete.

"Get this—" Liz began, breathless. She'd had to run across Mrs. Muleford's lawn to catch him. "Harold Muleford spent the night with Mrs. Muleford."

Alton shot her a weird glance.

"I went around back," she explained, as if stating the obvious. "I tried the gate."

"And ran into The Man From Glad," Alton finished for

her, taking a left turn without pausing at all for the stop sign.

"Right," Liz said. "And he told me Muleford spent the night. Apparently he does from time to time."

Alton didn't say a word. She seemed unreasonably proud of herself.

"What's wrong with that?" Liz wanted to know, offended by his brooding silence. "Muleford couldn't have killed Jennings, don't you see?"

Still, Alton said nothing. He'd thought he'd been in charge of things and, now, it was clear to him that Isabel Buddery was out of his control. How could he keep her safe if she insisted on jumping out of the van every time he came to stop? She was going to get herself killed.

"I mean, why would Hans lie about it?"

"Why the hell not?"

"Because nobody knows that Jennings is dead," Liz said angrily.

"Somebody knows," Alton emphasized. "And just where did you learn to interview people concerning the whereabouts of a suspect at the time a murder took place?"

"I suppose I come by it naturally. I have an interest in this, you know. I wanted to find out if the man I was working for was clean. I'd hate to think I was used to set up someone for murder. That's all."

A long silence followed.

"We're not playing games, Liz," Alton spat. "This is life and death, okay?"

"Well, what did you find out?" she asked, undaunted by Alton's little lecture.

"Not a damn thing." He pulled into a filling station to use the public telephone. "And don't you think that alibi of Muleford's is a bit too pat? If you ask me, it's exactly what a murderer would do, set up an alibi like that." He climbed out of the van, taking his keys.

"Stay put," he ordered, before slamming the door.

Jennings' murder had been planned. A man who would plan a murder would also plan an alibi. Didn't she understand anything?

"Yes?" James Spivey said, answering his phone with a simple question to which there was no answer.

"Sorry I missed our date," Alton said. "Something came up."

"Where is it, Franklin?" Spivey asked, his voice rising an octave as he realized it was Alton. "Just where the hell is the car?"

"Take it easy," Alton advised. "The car's safe. It's just that I'm not able at this point . . ."

"What are you trying to pull?" Spivey yelled, cutting him off. "You don't know what you're messing with, Franklin. I want that car delivered. And I want it now, do you understand me?"

"You're yodeling, Spivey. I won't talk to a man who's yodeling."

"Up yours!" the young attorney screeched. "If you think—"

"I want to know who I'm working for," Alton said, taking his turn to interrupt. "That's the bottom line."

"What?"

"Who I'm working for. Who hired Sargent to pay me to steal the car? Who gets the car when I deliver it to you? Am I going too fast for you, counselor?"

"Not on your life, Franklin," Spivey said, laying down the law. Alton hung up on him. He counted to ten and redialed the number.

"See how easy that is?" Alton asked when Spivey answered the phone.

"We can find you, Franklin. We can find you if we have to."

"But you don't have to," Alton announced cordially. "I'll give you the car. A deal's a deal, right? I just want to know who it's for."

"There's no time for this," Spivey said.

Alton hung up. This time he waited a few minutes. Liz sat primly in the passenger seat of the van, watching him. Alton had two more quarters. The afternoon paper was in the stand.

"Last chance," Alton told Spivey, who picked it up in the midst of the first ring. "I'm using my last quarter to buy a paper."

"Hold on," Spivey pleaded. "Just hold on, will you? Give me a second to think."

"I told you I'm all out of change. Who hired us to get the car?"

"Harold Muleford," Spivey said plainly. "And I don't want to hear from you that it makes a damn bit of difference. Now, we can't move the car in the daylight, but twenty minutes after sunset the SS 100 X is going to show up where it's supposed . . ."

Alton hung up. Keeping Spivey nervous was the only fun left in this misadventure.

Was it feasible, he wondered, that Harold Muleford had hired Sargent Security to procure the car while simultaneously planting Isabel Buddery as his "inside man" at the auction? Spivey hadn't pulled the name out of a hat. And Spivey wasn't, Alton was convinced, lying. Alton absentmindedly rubbed his right eye.

It was feasible. The bulldog who'd pulled off that dummy duel would have had six people bidding for him on the car if he could have managed it. Alton and Liz had been working together all along. And, now, it was time he confronted their boss. As long as Alton had control of the car, everyone stayed alive.

He used his last quarter to call the room at the Alameda. He shouldn't have treated Monique that way. He called to say something nice, something encouraging. He called to tell her everything would be okay. No one answered. And that wasn't okay. Alton cursed. Why wouldn't women listen to him anymore? It was for their own good.

Alton dumped chili on two do-it-yourself hot dogs at the 7-Eleven. He bought a family-size bag of potato chips and two large diet sodas, after finding a plastic hairbrush for $3.25 next to the disposable lighters. He had to make three trips to the van to carry out everything. And he nearly forgot to pick up a copy of the *Kansas City Star.*

They ate their late lunch without comment, watching the people come and go at the convenience store.

"Aren't you dying of curiosity?" Liz wanted to know. "If you aren't going to read the thing, give it to me."

Alton wolfed down his last bite and handed her the paper.

"Find the article and read it to me," he suggested.

He started the van and drove out of the parking lot, using his side mirror to narrowly miss scraping the side of a long, tan car parked too close to them. After scanning the front page, Liz removed the "Metropolitan Section." It seemed wrong to her that the theft of President Kennedy's limousine hadn't made the front page of every newspaper in the country.

She read the headline aloud: *Natural Gas Explosion Damages Local Residence.*

Liz glanced quickly up at Alton. "You ignited the gas line?"

"Just read the story," Alton said. "And don't believe everything you read."

For Alton, hearing the newscopy read aloud was his return to the scene of the crime. If the fireplace had had one of those gas starters, it might explain the paper's conclusion. Surely, the police didn't believe that. Or did they?

"No one was home at the time of the explosion," Liz read. "Forrest Jennings, local philanthropist, who lives at the residence was said by acquaintances to be out of the country."

"That's a nice way of putting it," Alton piped in.

"Listen to this," Liz urged. "Harold Muleford, president and owner of Kansas City–based Jack Rabbit Transit, has authorized repair of the structure in Mr. Jennings' absence. Mr. Muleford, a longtime friend of Mr. Jennings, said that the Gas Service Company completed an investigation of the early morning explosion and found an incorrectly installed fire-log starter to be at fault."

"He's covering up the theft," Alton said. "Now, tell me that man's not the murderer!"

"It gets better." Liz continued to read.

"Gregory Wright, a gardener shared by Mr. Jennings and Mr. Muleford, was on the premises of the Jennings estate when the explosion occurred. 'It was plenty scary,' Mr. Wright told reporters. 'I jumped in one of Mr. Jennings' cars and drove to get help right away. It was like a bomb going off.'

"A Kansas City Fire Department spokesman said there was a definite threat of fire when they arrived on the scene shortly after the blast, but that the explosion had blown out the original fire. Gas Service Company employees shut down the natural gas feed to the residence within minutes of the explosion."

"This guy is good," Alton said. "Damn good. He covered everything. Even the pickup truck."

"It sure lets you off the hook. The police aren't even involved."

"Don't kid yourself about my being off the hook. If I was a suspect in a car theft, my murder would arouse suspicion. This way, Muleford can do with me what he wants to. All he's after is that car. And he made damn sure nobody knows it's missing, not to mention Forrest Jennings himself."

Alton pulled onto Truman Memorial to cut across town to the east side, where the offices of Jack Rabbit Transit were stacked neatly to one side of the largest tractor-trailer warehouse in four states. He slipped the hairbrush from the pocket of his windbreaker and handed it to Liz.

"Thanks," she said with genuine appreciation and began to brush back her dark hair.

"If there's anything else you need, just let me know."

"A toothbrush and toothpaste," she said wearily. "A bath, deodorant, eyeliner and about a twenty-year nap."

"What about Barnett?" Alton wondered aloud. "Where the hell was Barnett in that story? Was he there last night?"

"Yes; he lives there. And he seemed awfully loyal to Jennings."

"Or maybe he was a plant. Maybe he was working for Muleford, too. Speaking of which, how did you get set up with the bald bulldog anyway?" Alton seriously doubted that Jennings' personal bodyguard worked for Muleford. But the two millionaires had apparently been baiting each other for decades. Barnett might have been in place as an ally of Muleford for years.

"Met him at a party," Liz said offhandedly. "Harold liked my looks. A few weeks later I received a telephone call. He said he had a job for me."

"Did it pay well?"

"Not when you consider that I lost my earrings to that friend of yours. I'd say I'm in the red on this one." Liz dusted a potato chip crumb from the knee of her black slacks.

"How did it work? Did Muleford fill you in on the car?"

"Not really. He told me there was a car of course. But it was Jennings who did all the talking. He showed it to me. More than once."

"How did you know about the bidders, that Feigen was CIA? Did Muleford do the research on that?"

"No. It was Jennings again. He was smart. He'd done

all his homework, but he liked to talk. He thought a woman couldn't hurt him, I guess."

"And you took it all in. Had you talked to Muleford since the auction?"

"No," Liz said with a touch of spite in her voice. "When do I get off the witness stand? I didn't steal the car. You did."

"True," Alton said. "But you would have, wouldn't you?"

"It's funny," Liz said. "But, you know, when I was bidding, I believed I was actually buying it. After seeing the car, it became very special to me. It was as if I were buying it for myself."

"So your bid was a legitimate one?"

"Of course. Muleford didn't like having to, but he would have paid for the car."

"We're here to see that he does," Alton said with unwarranted bravado. "I don't like killers. One way or the other, he's going to pay. I'm going to wave that stinking car under his nose and I promise you one thing. I'll blow the damn thing up or drive it into the Missouri River before Harold Muleford gets his hands on it."

"There are other options," Liz said, thinking of alternate places the SS 100 X could end up.

"It would make a fancy planter at that. Think you could fit it inside your apartment?"

"Hey, who said I live in an apartment?"

"I looked you up when we were at the department store. You're in the book."

"Under *L*. It could be Larry Buddery you looked up."

"Liz, there's only one Buddery listed in Kansas City. And a man never has his phone number listed under his first initial. It's you."

"Did you call the number?"

"What if I did?"

"You'd have reached a machine, that's what," Liz said. "With a man's voice on it."

"So tell me what you do for a living," Alton requested.

"I don't steal cars," she said.

"Seriously. I'd hate to have to tie you up."

"You'd love it," Liz snapped, her eyes on fire.

"You're avoiding the question."

"I live off my assets. It's not all that difficult."

She was lying. It was a clever way of lying, Alton realized, but lying nonetheless. Maybe she didn't want him dropping by the office where she was executive secretary this or computer specialist that. Maybe she just didn't want a thief and a gambler knowing all that much about her. She was practiced at keeping her distance. Isabel Buddery was born aloof. But it wasn't as if he were asking her to fall in love with him.

Alton checked his mirrors and eased into the left lane to pass a Metro bus. Instantly, a small car lay on its irritating horn, swerving, and Alton jerked the steering wheel to the right.

"Blind spot," he apologized.

"Blind spot, bullshit," Liz said. "You were looking at me."

"Same thing," Alton said.

Alton's gaze met the marble eyes of a stuffed jackrabbit in a glass box in the paneled lobby of Harold Muleford's trucking company. A slight man behind a pile of bills of lading ignored Alton's entry as effectively as the taxidermied Bugs Bunny. Behind a deep desktop sat a portly woman in her fifties. She wore a severe shade of rouge and no other makeup. Her dark gray hair was tied up to either side of her head and to Alton she resembled a moose.

"Mr. Muleford, please," he said.

Mrs. Bullwinkle stared hard at him. Alton must not have looked like the regular run of cartoon characters through the office. The moose lady said nothing.

Neither did she appear about to move.

"I'm here to see Mr. Muleford," Alton tried again, a bit more animated. If there was a smile on her face it was hidden in a slight tic at the very corner of her mouth done up with the dark, thin hairs of a mustache.

She blinked. Things were rolling now. Then she slowly pushed back her chair. It was a matter of timing, Alton realized. The moose lady had all day to kill and so few tasks to accomplish that she no doubt had developed over the days, months and years this skilled slow-motion routine. It served to expand even the simplest chore to fill the time between lunch and her afternoon coffee break.

"I'm here on behalf of Forrest Jennings and I'm certain Mr. Muleford would very much like to see me. Right now."

In the time it took to lift herself from the chair there was ample time to book a dozen bets on whether or not she would. Eventually, she disappeared inside a door behind her desk, closing it after she entered. She and Elmer Fudd needed their privacy, Alton figured.

He snatched up one of the two telephones on her desk and punched out the number of the Alameda. "Hopping to Please, my ass," Alton mumbled. The clerk at the other desk coughed and Alton guessed he was stifling a laugh. No one answered the call.

Alton's best hope was that Monique had discovered the enclosed pool on the roof of the Alameda Plaza Hotel and was enjoying an afternoon drink with a splash of chlorine in the air. He put the call through again and let it ring, losing count.

CHAPTER FOURTEEN

Harold Muleford at work was everything Alton had expected. And worse.

He sported a plaid flannel shirt and green corduroy pants held up with a scarred brown belt tucked in neatly under the swell of his gut. He smoked a cigar. Since Christopher Columbus discovered Cuba, they hadn't made one of those yet that didn't stink. Muleford's office was smaller but reminded Alton of a bar in a bowling alley. All that was missing was the fat-hipped bleached blonde and a couple neon beer signs.

The carpet was orange shag. The chair and couch were upholstered in blue velveteen, worn a soft green on the arms and the edges of the cushions. If Harold Muleford collected art, none of it cluttered up his office. Unless you considered the Jack Rabbit Transit calendar featuring a high-heeled bathing beauty to be art.

Working here was Donald Trump's personal vision of hell. From Alton's view, it probably beat being in jail, given the too large air conditioner stuck in the middle of one wall of cheap, plastic paneling.

"What is it, young man?" Muleford stood behind the desk, staring right through Alton. Muleford didn't look like the guy who'd just beaten you out of the rent on Baltic Avenue in real-life Monopoly. Except for his eyes. They weren't so much piercing as they were damaging. You judged yourself in Muleford's stare and came up short.

"I'm here about the car."

"Yeah, you were at the auction last night."

Muleford's stare changed into a look of closer appraisal. Somebody else might have hotels on Park Place and Broadway, own the utilities and all four railroads; but Alton had the car.

"Well, what did you think, son?" Muleford sat his fat ass down behind his desk. "Pretty good, wouldn't you say?"

"What's that?"

"The duel!" the bulldog nearly shouted. "Did I have him shitting his pants or what? You, too, probably."

Muleford glanced away, chuckling, once Alton agreed that the bald man's mock duel had been effective. Apparently Muleford had seen all he needed to in Alton's response to his question.

"About the car," Alton said. "I'm the guy you hired to bid on it for you."

"Is that so?" Muleford asked rhetorically, puffing on his cigar. "And how much did I pay you, son?"

"A hundred thousand."

Muleford's eyes danced, like darts looking for a place to land. Then he laughed.

"I'm afraid somebody's been putting you on," Muleford said. "If you're here to collect your pay, you can stick your head up your ass and look for it there and do about as good."

Alton remembered the way Muleford had handled the explosion for the papers. Surely, he knew that Alton had already been paid. Muleford was playing dumb, snatching up the "Get Out of Jail Free" card and holding on to it just to keep you from getting it.

"I've already been paid. I don't want money."

"And who paid you?"

"You did. Up front."

Muleford laughed again. It was a mirthless chuckle. "You've been had, son. But if you've been paid, what's the beef?"

"You also hired me to steal the car if I could, if the bid

was not accepted." Alton felt like an idiot for being forced to tell Muleford his own terms. This time the fat man didn't laugh. He rested his cigar in an ashtray and put both hands on his desk.

"Your name's Franklin, right? Well, have a seat Mr. Franklin."

Alton settled into the chair, wary. Harold Muleford stood from his desk and walked to a curtained window to one side of the room.

"Are you telling me you stole the car?" Muleford asked, his back to Alton.

"No, sir. Somebody beat me to it."

"They sure did get up early today, didn't they?" Muleford turned from the window. "Then tell me, son, what the hell are you doing here?"

Alton wondered if he should stand. He saw nothing to be gained in being confrontational. He leaned forward slightly in the chair. "Forrest Jennings is dead and I think you might have killed him."

There was a long silence while Muleford favored Alton with one of his more menacing stares.

"Have I ever met you?"

"No, sir." Alton saw no reason not to be polite. "James Spivey arranged everything. He hired me on your behalf."

"Spivey?" Muleford growled. "I don't know any Spivey. Never heard of him."

"He's an attorney with Sargent Security. Perhaps you worked this out with Ray Sargent himself, but I'm what you ended up with."

"You got balls," Muleford said without making the statement sound in any way like a compliment. "Ray Sargent finds out you're spreading this kind of bullshit around town you could be in real trouble."

"I'm already in trouble," Alton confessed, tired of Muleford's well-acted charade. "I'm afraid that whoever killed Jennings won't let it stop there. I just want to be let off the hook."

"Okay, stop!" Muleford plopped back down in his chair and stared at something on his desk. The stocky millionaire spoke slowly, picking up his cigar: "Now, let's say that there was a murder, which I don't believe there was. But let's say there was a murder. Wouldn't the person who stole the car be the one who killed him?"

"I believe you stole the car." It might be the one lie that would throw Muleford offtrack. Perhaps he'd mistrust Spivey at this point if Alton convinced Muleford that he hadn't stolen the SS 100 X. Spivey of course would tell him otherwise.

"Forget that," Muleford ordered. "I don't want that damn car. I never wanted that car. I just wanted Forrest to believe that I wanted it." He puffed a small cloud of malodorous smoke, then continued.

"You see, son, Mr. Jennings and I—well, we go way back. You might say we're rivals. Now he's a sharp one, you should understand that. It isn't easy to get the best of Forrest Jennings. Especially when he knows you're trying.

"He'll jerk the damn rug right out from under your feet before you even know you're standing on it. He's quick, awfully quick."

Muleford stroked his cigar, slowing down the performance to make it stick. Alton played along by keeping his mouth shut.

"Now, if you truly believe Forrest Jennings is dead, it's because he wants you to believe he's dead. You're in over your head, young man. Do you understand me?"

Alton nodded obliquely, recalling the condition of the body he'd lifted from the trunk of the SS 100 X. There was nothing alive about it and if Jennings wasn't dead it was a trick on God, not on Alton. Jennings might have been sharp, all right; but it took more than cunning to pull off a resurrection.

"If I was in your shoes, I'd clear out and settle up. Jennings has you dangling and you might as well cut the string yourself."

They were nearing the end of Muleford's one-act drama and his cigar. Alton had promised himself not to mention Isabel Buddery. She was the one Muleford was after and it was clear now that there'd be no dealing with Harold Muleford. For the time being, the bulldog man remained impenetrable.

"I can see why you might think I'd kill Forrest. Hell, you probably thought he was dead last night at about the same time he did. That duel was one of my best moves." Harold Muleford smiled. It was about as charming as his laugh. He stubbed out the slimy end of his fat cigar.

"But I like a good game," the trucking magnate went on. "And Forrest, why he's the best game in town. Now, if I was to kill my best enemy, there wouldn't be much left for me to do. There wouldn't be anybody left worth the fight." There was something poignantly sincere in Muleford's speech, Alton realized, something as sincere as secret regret.

Once Alton had left, Harold Muleford grabbed the telephone and slowly punched off a local number from memory. "I know who killed the son of a bitch," he said into the receiver. "And I think we'd better do something about it."

CHAPTER FIFTEEN

Alton was enraged. Liz had slipped out of the van again.

He wasn't sure who to believe or what to believe, but he was sure of one thing. Whoever killed Forrest Jennings needed to kill Isabel Buddery. They'd made a mistake in not killing her that night. And now Alton probably needed to be killed himself. Also, he gravely suspected that Monique was in danger. It didn't make for a good mood on a bright and sunny April afternoon.

Having stared long enough at the empty living area of the converted van, Alton jumped out from behind the steering wheel, swiveling the captain's chair with a bang. He saw Liz coming out from behind Muleford's office building. He was livid, jogging to meet her in the middle of the parking lot. A semi roared through in low gear, stealing all other sound.

Alton grabbed her by the arm and jerked violently in the direction of the van.

"Let go of me!" Liz screamed. He slapped her hard with his left hand and continued dragging her toward the van. Liz collapsed within herself and ceased to struggle. Alton's palm stung.

"Not a word," he demanded, swinging open the passenger door to shove her up and in. "Not a single word!"

Quick-stepping around the front of the van, Alton's anger only increased. He was angry at himself for hitting her, but more incensed at her reckless behavior. Alton started the engine without talking, squealed in reverse and drove out of the lot as rapidly as first and second gears would allow. He had it in third when he spun sharply onto Truman Memorial, tossing Liz against the passenger door.

An Oldsmobile honked. Alton cursed the driver and thrust his arm out the window, the middle finger pointing out the clear, blue sky.

"Damn you," Liz said softly. "Damn you, damn you."

The van slipped through changing traffic lights, heading back toward the center of town. Alton turned south on the Paseo, raced along for three more blurred blocks, then stepped on the brakes for a sharp right turn onto a side street.

"Shut up," he said. Alton rubbed his face with his hand, trying to calm down, trying to bring the pieces of his self-control back together after they exploded in Muleford's parking lot.

"I had to go to the bathroom and I was . . ."

"Shut up and listen." Liz's head was down, her shoulders slumped. Her dark hair fell forward, blocking her face from view. Alton knew it hurt.

"You need a proper reality," he said. "You're . . ." Alton stopped. His voice was shaking. "You're going to get us both killed.

"I don't want you dead, Liz. And I sure as hell don't want me dead either."

She wouldn't look up. The burning of his hand felt ugly. He squeezed his eyes shut tight for a moment, the right one still itchy from the dose of gunpowder he'd rubbed into it that morning.

"You *can* die, you know," he said, looking out his window at a row of apartment windows in a brick building. "Everybody can. Every six minutes somebody dies by accident in this country. Every six minutes! And nobody wanted them dead, Liz. And nobody wanted to die. It just happens. Read the papers.

"You aren't any different from them. You're not better. You're no more valuable to anybody than they are. You aren't more religious. You aren't any smarter. And you aren't richer. None of that crap matters. Accidents kill the worthy and the unworthy alike."

Alton took a deep breath. The words were coming out of him from somewhere he couldn't control.

"That's bad enough. You're lucky every time six minutes go by and you're still alive. That's the prize and you win it ten times an hour, every hour, every day, whether you're awake or asleep, drunk or sober. You win the prize until you lose. Everything. Then it's over."

"Is that your sermon?" she said through clenched teeth, her head still bowed. "Are you quite through?"

"No, I'm not, dammit!" He wondered if he was talking to her or to himself. Alton wanted to say he was sorry for hitting her, but he wasn't ready yet.

"I can't think of a nice way to die. It's lonely. And it's painful to know it's happening. God, it's got to hurt to die. But, Liz, I don't want to be surprised either."

She was listening now. Alton knew that Isabel Buddery could pop open her door and walk if she really wanted to. He didn't know if he would try to stop her.

He thought of President Kennedy riding in the far backseat of that 1961 Lincoln Continental convertible. It was such a dark blue that even some of the newsmen at the scene had called it black. He saw the young president's arm going to his neck after the first rifle shot. Alton shook his thoughts and came clean.

"Dying by accident is bad enough," he said, "but when somebody wants to kill you, it gets worse. Please listen to me. Somebody not only wants to kill you, somebody *needs* to kill you. That's a big difference.

"Somebody in this city, who knows who you are, who loaded you into the trunk of that car, needs to kill you. Can't you understand? And he knows how to kill and he's killed before, just last night. He's got nothing to lose by killing you and plenty to gain.

"He's looking for you, lady. Don't think for a second that he isn't. He finds you now and there's no stopping it.

Nobody's going to throw his body between the two of you just as Eliot Ness rounds the corner and blows the bad guy away. When somebody who knows how needs to kill you, your life's a distant long shot fading in the backstretch."

Liz straightened in the passenger seat. Alton looked at her carefully. He wanted very badly to touch her gently. He didn't want to be a threat in her life and he didn't want her to hate him. She'd been crying. He had no idea whether she was crying from the pain of his having slapped her or from anger. Or for some other reason he couldn't fathom.

A small corner of her upper lip had swelled. But it would stop hurting soon enough. Anyway, for her it would.

After pushing through several blocks of dreary silence between the two of them, Alton had the van on Broadway, heading toward Westport from Thirty-first Street.

"Now that you're through beating on me, do you mind telling me where we're going?"

"Be nice," he said from force of habit.

"That's cute," Liz said venomously. "And if I'm not, are you going to spank me—with a switch, out behind the woodshed maybe."

Alton reached out his hand and rested it momentarily on her leg. It was a simple gesture, a touch of kindness.

"What the hell is that? A little pat on the leg and everything's supposed to be okay. Listen, Mr. Franklin, I hate men who hit women for their own good. I hate them."

"I'm sorry." It was the only time, though, he would say it. Later, when she went back over things, it would be there. That's all that mattered.

"I once met a guy from South Africa," Alton said. "Davis Makande. He was a native of one tribe or the other, you know, with those parallel scars on his face that look like plow tracks. He was six-six easy, big guy. And he

spoke with a Bishop Tutu accent. It'd break you up to
hear him talk."

"Only if you've never been to South Africa," Liz said,
hoping to insult him. Alton ignored the remark.

"Among his people, they had this tradition that whenever two people quarreled it would be ended by them
touching each other. One of them would reach out and,
in the middle of the fight, touch the other one and that
was that. The anger lifted."

"We have the same tradition," Liz informed him. "It's
called shaking hands."

Alton turned right on Forty-seventh, driving through
the heart of the Country Club Plaza, past the tennis
courts, the stucco and tile Spanish buildings, the fountains and the statues.

"If you're going back to your hotel, you missed your
turn," Liz said. A convertible Volkswagen stopped suddenly in front of them to allow a group of pedestrians to
cross in the middle of the block. Alton was accustomed to
this Midwestern courtesy and eased safely to a stop behind the white VW.

"You know, I've never yet seen one of those VW convertibles that wasn't driven by a good-looking woman. I
think all the dealerships got together and agreed to only
sell white VW convertibles to college coeds and to the
cheerleaders' fathers. You get one of those for your sixteenth birthday, you know you're pretty."

"So where are we going, wise guy? That is, if I'm allowed to know."

"Your apartment. I looked it up in the phone book,
remember?"

Liz let it sink in. "Do you think it's safe?" she asked,
hoping that he wouldn't.

"Very," Alton said.

He parked in front of the Russell Lowell Building on
Brush Creek Parkway. Alton removed the keys and
opened his door. Liz stayed glued to her seat.

"You coming?"

"I don't have a key. Let's see if you make it in alive, first."

"Be right back then." When Alton was halfway across the crisp lawn in front of the apartment building, she rolled down the window and called to him.

"What?" he asked innocently.

"Get back in the van," Liz said, knowing she'd been caught.

Alton returned to his seat behind the steering wheel and eased the door closed, replacing the key in the ignition.

"How did you know?" she asked.

"When you asked me to take you home this morning, you knew I wouldn't do it. Then there was that stuff about your answering machine. You seemed bothered by the fact I might have called your number. That is, I might have called L. Buddery's number. So—where are you from?"

"Chicago," Liz replied. "Born and raised."

"What hotel are you in?"

"Does it matter?"

"Yes."

"Westin Crown Center."

"Feigen's hotel?"

"Well, it's not like he owns it or anything. But I found out at the auction that he was staying there. Jennings told me. For a while, that bothered him. He thought Feigen and I were in cahoots."

"Cahoots?" Alton asked as if stricken. "Do they say that in Chicago?"

"Don't be an ass," Liz said as he pulled out into traffic.

"Well, are you?" he asked. "In cahoots, I mean?"

"No," Liz stated summarily. "Look, the less you knew about me, the less anybody knew about me, the better. All right? I met Muleford in Chicago. He flew me down to bid on the car. That's all I know."

"And what Jennings told you."

"Like I said, he filled me in on people."

"Liz, if Jennings had the line on everyone else at the auction, he surely knew all about you."

"I realize that. Maybe he was supposed to. Maybe Muleford just wanted an audience for his little duel. Maybe he didn't kill Jennings. What did he tell you?"

"Nothing. I come up empty everywhere I turn. He said he didn't know who I was for one thing. He said he didn't know the go-between who hired me for him. Said he'd never heard of him, in fact. And he said he had no interest in the car whatsoever at this point."

"Figures," Liz said. "He's no idiot, Frankie."

"But maybe I am. Hell, he pretended not to know that Jennings was dead and he did a good job of it. I couldn't get to him from any angle."

"Did you mention me?"

Alton wondered why she asked, then decided it was a reasonable question.

"No. I'm still trying to figure out my role in all of this. Spivey may have just dropped his name in an emergency. I don't know who the hell I'm working for."

"Who's Spivey?" Liz asked.

"That, young lady, is exactly what I aim to find out."

But Spivey would have to wait.

Monique's situation demanded immediate attention. Going over the room, Alton might be able to discern whether she'd gone on a jaunt of her own or somebody had abducted her. Perhaps she had returned by now, but other thoughts kept intruding—unpleasant thoughts. A lurid picture of Monique tied with heavy ropes to a chair under a dangling, bare light bulb, her clothes in shreds, had imprinted itself on Alton's mind.

It was those damned men's magazines from his youth that gave him the picture, magazine covers he'd sneaked looks at on the drugstore racks when his mother had told him he could pick out a comic book. Yet, the threat to Monique was potentially very real.

Alton was through playing games. With Liz's hesitant cooperation, he had her lie down on the bed in the back of the converted van. From one of the built-in cabinets, he came up with a pair of police-issue handcuffs.

Careful not to tighten the steel cuff on her wrist where it would bite the skin, Alton affixed the other cuff around the center post of the small table in the van. The post was bolted to the floor. Unless Liz could use her teeth as an adjustable crescent wrench, she'd be there when he got back.

Lying down, she had to stay on her back or side, but Liz would be able to sit up if she wanted to.

"I shouldn't be too long," Alton told her.

"I can use the nap," Liz said. "You sure you don't want to beat me senseless before you leave?"

Of all the things Alton wanted to do to her, that wasn't one of them. At the moment.

He blew her a kiss and crawled up front, drawing the curtain. All of this of course would be impossible to explain to Monique. But she should be pleased to discover that Isabel Buddery was now his captive and not his companion when he brought Monique back to the van and abandoned the Alameda Plaza Hotel altogether.

Rick Feigen met him in the lobby. He purposefully cut Alton off on his way to the elevators.

"They're in your room," the white-haired gentleman said in a hushed warning. Alton's heart hit bottom.

"Who?" Alton met the older man's determined gaze.

"I don't know. But there are two of them."

"How long?"

"More than an hour now," Feigen said, glancing at his watch. He smiled at Alton then, and added, "You should have talked to me sooner."

"Not now," Alton said, his mind spinning. He turned

sharply away from the CIA agent and rushed the front desk of the Alameda.

"Two men are robbing my room," Alton told the clerk and gave her his room number, the room reserved in his name, the room he hoped to hell the men had chosen to stake out.

"I don't understand," the girl said, stammering in her prim white blouse and black string tie. "Are you certain?"

"Call security—*now,*" Alton barked. "And get the whole crew up there."

"Yes of course," she said.

"Now!" he shouted. "I've alerted you to a robbery in progress. If nothing is done about it this instant, I'll sue you first thing tomorrow morning for gross negligence. Your hotel will settle out of court by mid-afternoon and your ass will be canned that evening."

She picked up the telephone.

CHAPTER SIXTEEN

Nothing about their appearance was startling.

From the end of the hall, Alton watched four security guards and two Kansas City uniformed police officers escort the two men into the elevator. They could have worked for anybody. The duo looked as much like two junior college football players dressed up for the annual All-Sports Banquet as young henchmen in the employ of Jack Soo & Associates. Alton couldn't see any blood on their hands.

"We'll need a list of everything that's missing," the assistant hotel manager said. Alton looked around the room. It wasn't as messy as when he'd left it this morning. Their clothes had been put away and the beds were made.

"Of course they'll be searched," the head of security told him. "Was there any cash in the room?"

"Nothing's missing," Alton said, considering his options. The two hotel employees looked questioningly at each other. They didn't want to call the whole thing off. But Alton would just as soon the two men left his room. He needed to check out the room across the hall.

"The police will need you to sign a complaint," the security man said. "You'll need to drop by the Linwood Station. Do you know where that is?"

"We'd be happy to send 'round a car," his co-worker offered.

"Either way, we've got them on criminal trespass," the other bragged. "Even if nothing's missing."

"Not breaking and entering?" Alton said.

"Apparently the maid let them into the room," the security man said knowingly. He held out his left hand, palm up, and rubbed his thumb across his fingertips. Alton considered the advantages to ripping off hotel rooms. There was far less risk, it seemed, than in stealing cars.

"Then you can sign the complaint," Alton told the assistant manager.

"I suppose so. Is that right, Bill?"

The security man nodded. "But please go through your things carefully," he requested. "We must be certain that nothing's missing."

Only a dark-eyed cocktail waitress in her mid-twenties was missing, he wanted to say. Alton was told that the Alameda hoped he enjoyed the remainder of his stay in Kansas City and that the hotel would be more than pleased to pick up his bill through the end of the week.

"I'd rather you didn't," Alton said and both men exchanged looks again. The tab on this room was Spivey's and Alton wasn't giving anything away.

"We have complimentary box seats available to tonight's Royals-Yankees game," the assistant manager said. "The hotel would be pleased to provide transportation."

"I hate the Yankees," Alton said, realizing that it was this man's job to offer Alton something. Next, he'd be told to keep the towels and wooden coat hangers.

Once the two men left, Alton looked in the closet and the bathroom. Her clothes were gone. His were still there, including the rented tuxedo and the black patent-leather shoes.

Alton darted across the hall and, after fumbling with the key, discovered no bare light bulb, no rope and no torn clothes. This room had been cleaned, too. The dishes had been removed and new glasses sat on a tray on the table. Under the bottle of scotch, Alton found a hotel envelope with his name written on it.

Alton opened it. He unscrewed the cap from the scotch and took two sips. Monique had left him, the note said, and she promised to pay him back someday for the money she'd taken. It was the best news he'd had all day.

Downstairs, Rick Feigen had faded into the shadows. Alton didn't have time to look for him. As Alton hurried back to the van, he expected the white-haired fellow to jump out from behind one of the concrete posts in the parking garage. He didn't.

But Alton had another surprise. Liz was sitting in the front passenger seat, the loosened handcuffs in her lap.

"Is your girlfriend all right?" Liz wanted to know as Alton climbed behind the steering wheel. She'd asked the right question; Alton had to give her that much.

"She left town and she should be fine. Unless they picked her up on her way to the bus station."

"Why didn't she fly?"

"It probably didn't occur to her," was all Alton could think to say. He started the van. "How'd you get the cuffs off?"

"The key was in the cabinet. It wasn't hard to reach."

Alton backed out of the end slot, using both side mirrors.

"And now I'm supposed to trust you, is that it?"

"Well, I didn't run away."

"You want the car," he accused, realizing it was true. "Maybe you didn't to begin with, but you want it now."

Liz didn't say anything.

"I'd advise you to give up on that idea," Alton said.

He drove to the Kansas side and headed south, away from town. The suburban office parks were all the rage now and it was time he paid one of the short-stack company buildings a visit. On the way, Alton told her about the henchmen waiting in his room, leaving out the part about Rick Feigen tipping him off.

"Who were they?" Liz asked.

"Hired hands is all I know. Could be working for any-one."

"You didn't ask them?"

"I didn't talk to them. They had guns."

"Did they have permits?"

"Yes. Still, they could be anyone. They weren't carry-ing cards that named their employer. But, if you want to go down to the police station, we can probably find out."

"No, thank you."

"They could have been federal agents, for all I know, not wanting to blow their cover," Alton went on, think-ing of Rick Feigen. Alton mentally flipped a coin. It was Muleford. It was Spivey. It was Muleford and Spivey. On the umpteenth flip, it came up Jack Soo. The fourth possibility bothered him most of all.

After several blocks of tree-dappled late-afternoon sunshine along Nall Avenue, Liz piped up.

"How about you? Do you have a gun?"

"You mean you didn't find one in the back when you were rummaging around?"

Alton was no longer on parole from the time he'd spent in an Oklahoma state pen, but from sea to shining sea in this country of spacious skies and narrow, dark alleyways, the police still frowned on convicted felons having guns. Stealing cars in past years had never meant needing one; though, suddenly it seemed staying alive depended on it.

For the right price, Meza could procure anything Al-ton wanted. Alton thought of a better way.

Corporate Woods had just a decade ago been some-body's dying pasture on the southern edge of the Kansas City metropolitan area. Now, the cows were gone, but there was plenty of bullshit lying around the place. Cor-porate Woods was a theme park for so-called adults.

The barn and silo had been replaced by a dozen or so twenty-story buildings cast at angles among marked jog-ging trails. It looked to Alton like what you'd get if you turned a carnival funhouse inside out and enlarged it by ten. All the offices had views of the scattered trees, the joggers, the creek. But mostly they had views of each other and the parking lots.

The reflection of one building upon the exterior glass wall of another looked grotesquely fat, then thin and curvy as you drove nearer.

Alton circled one building, located the reserved parking spaces along one side, just off the front entrance. He parked nearby, where he could watch the cars there and the magic doors that opened as you approached.

Liz relented to having her left wrist handcuffed to the steering wheel.

"Who lives here?" she asked.

"Just watch my back," Alton said. "I'll be right out."

"What am I supposed to do? I don't have the keys."

"Honk."

In the lobby were two elevators, a company sign etched into lighted glass, and expensively framed greeting-card art. They were the kind of pictures you wanted to stick a stamp on and mail to some relative after you'd forgotten his birthday but needed to borrow fifty bucks. This was the world of Sargent Security, Inc. Every inch of it.

There were plastic rest rooms off a short hall across from the security desk, as good a place as any for a retiree to read a magazine and call it a second career. The old guy wore a light blue uniform with patches on the sleeves, but it was apparent that 90 percent of his job was showing up. The other 10 percent involved offering visitors directory assistance. Alton wondered if Ray Sargent minded paying for the service it was his company's mission to supply for others.

He stood in the middle of the wide lobby and pantomimed dialing a telephone. The old man kindly threw a finger toward the hall with the public rest rooms. Alton had picked up plenty of change from the 7-Eleven fine-dining section when he'd treated Isabel Buddery to lunch. Now, he only needed a quarter.

"It's me," Alton said after he answered his direct line. "Glad I caught you."

"It's been a long day, Franklin," Spivey said as a caveat.

"The finest kind," Alton chirped. "Got a pencil handy?"

"Don't piss me off," Spivey warned.

"That's the last directive I'll take from you. If you want the car, here's what you're going to do. You don't want the car, hang up." Alton waited.

"Go ahead."

"I want the money in a briefcase, Spivey. And I want a gun."

"What? No way, Franklin."

"I don't give a damn whose gun. You can give me yours if you want. But it has to be loaded and the ammo had better be real. I'll test it before turning the car over."

"It can't be done. Why, I'd be a fool . . ."

"It can be done and it will be done. Right now."

"I'll see," Spivey compromised, always the lawyer. Alton suspected the call was being recorded.

"You're going to do this alone with nobody tailing you. I'll be watching. Now, write this down." And Alton told him where to go.

"I'm not sure it's worth the risk," Spivey said. "We didn't agree to you being paid up front. What's to keep you from taking the money and stiffing us."

Alton liked the way he said *us.*

"Ray Sargent," Alton said. "Or aren't you two keeping in touch?"

"I still don't like it," Spivey said again, stalling.

"Tough shit. It's the only bet you've got. You don't want the action, you can always go on home and call it quits. Otherwise, you've got about five minutes to get your ass in your car and get this thing over with. And don't forget the gun."

"Wait," Spivey requested. "Let's go over it again . . ."

Alton disconnected. He needed to use the rest room, but decided against it. Spivey could figure out Alton was in the building, if the young attorney looked out the right window. The last thing Alton wanted was to be trapped in a stall. He waved goodbye to the security desk on his way out of the building, as much for the benefit of the corner-mounted video cameras as for the old guy in permanent-press blues.

"Hello," Liz said when he climbed into the passenger side. "My turn to drive?"

"Just a second." Alton unlocked the captain's chair swivel, and slipped into the back of the van, drawing the curtain. In the cabinet, he found his trusty three-pound coffee can and pried off the plastic lid. In junior high school a teacher had told Alton that a pint's a pound the world around. He relieved himself a pound and a half worth into the metal can.

Climbing back up front, he opened the passenger door and set the lidded can on the parking lot.

"Did you have to be so loud?" she asked.

Alton started to say the noise was the result of the can when, straightening up, he caught sight of James Spivey walking rapidly to his car, briefcase in hand.

"Here," Alton said, handing her the keys. "Start it up."

"Is that Spivey?" she asked, inserting the key.

"Just follow that car and do what I say."

Spivey had spotted them. He tossed the briefcase into the front seat, got in, then sat with both hands on the steering wheel.

"You ever seen him before?" Alton asked.

"No. What's he waiting on?"

"Flash the lights."

"Where are they?"

Alton reached across her and flicked the knob to the

left side of the steering wheel. His arm brushed her breasts. Perhaps it was the building adrenaline, but Alton felt heat as his arm moved lightly across her sweater. Liz pretended not to notice.

Spivey pulled away. She popped the clutch, but the van didn't die. Letting her foot off the gas, they eased forward in second gear and trailed Spivey's car out of the parking lot, over the creek bridge and through the sparse woods, three trees deep.

"Dammit," Liz said. "Unlock me. I can't drive."

Alton was happy to oblige. He could use the heat. He tried not to lean into her too directly, but the contact was there as he unlocked the cuff from the steering wheel. He left it to dangle like an overgrown charm from the other bracelet he left secured around her arm.

"Have a good time?" she asked as he moved away from her.

"Just fine. Maybe sometime I'll ask you to dance."

"Maybe," Liz countered, "I won't turn you down." Her emphasis was on the *maybe*.

The traffic had thickened miserably by the time Spivey turned onto the ramp to I-35 North, following instructions. The two vehicles eased into the flow of traffic, Liz keeping the van a single car length behind.

"Why is he going so slow?"

"I told him to," Alton explained. "It's easier to spot a tail in traffic if you're going slower than the rest of the cars. Anybody who doesn't move into the other two lanes to pass you or who doesn't turn off at the next exit deserves attention."

"How the hell can you tell? I can't see behind me."

"The mirrors. It's all in the mirrors."

"Sure," she said skeptically. "What are we doing anyway?"

"Picking up my paycheck. Everybody has to eat."

"You sold the car?"

"I stole it for hire, Liz. Did you think I was going to keep it?"

She didn't respond, but stared straight ahead at Spivey's bumper.

"Besides, it's all in the family, according to Spivey. Muleford hedged his bets. He not only hired you, my dear, he engaged Sargent Security, who had the foresight to put their trust in me."

"You're not giving it to Muleford?" She flashed an alarmed look at Alton. He liked being looked at by those green eyes.

"Wasn't that the idea? Wasn't that the reason you were at the auction? Did something change your mind, Liz?"

"He doesn't deserve it."

"Well, it's not mine to give," Alton said. "Flash the lights."

Spivey put on his right turn signal and led them onto the Sixty-seventh Street exit ramp.

"Don't hit the turn signal," Alton instructed as they waited at a stop sign at the end of the ramp. "Flash the headlights again."

Spivey pulled through a hole in the cross traffic and drove straight along the access road which led into the parking lot of the Western Hills Motel. He slowed to a crawl and Liz and Alton were forced to wait for another gap to appear in the traffic on Sixty-seventh.

"Don't get too close." Alton reached across and sounded the horn three times. Spivey stopped along a row of vacant motel rooms fronting a hill. A chain-link fence kept children and dogs from slipping down the cliff onto I-35. Spivey, on his own volition, turned sharply and pulled up to the fence.

"Stop here," Alton said.

Liz pushed in the clutch and kept her other foot on the brake. They waited.

"Put it in reverse, just in case," Alton said, growing nervous.

"I can't back up," Liz protested. "I can't see."

But it didn't matter. Spivey stayed in the car. He leaned across the driver's seat and popped open the passenger door. His head disappeared momentarily as he closed the door after a pause. Spivey's gold-rimmed glasses glinted in the dying sunlight as he buckled his shoulder strap. Slowly, he backed away from the fence, his right arm across the top of the front seat. Then he drove toward them.

"Duck," Alton told her.

Spivey was playing the game by Alton's rules. He drove within five feet of the van as he pulled to the entrance of the parking lot off Sixty-seventh. He put on his emergency flashers and waited, watching them in his rear-view mirror.

"Take his place," Alton said as Liz straightened up in the seat. "Come on," he urged, tapping her on the leg with the back of his hand.

She pulled the van up to the chain-link fence and let it idle while Alton retrieved the tan briefcase Spivey had left on the parking lot pavement. As if a switch had been thrown, the sky turned a dull orange. Alton locked his door and counted the money.

"How much?" Liz asked.

"My fees are confidential."

"Really," she said. "I'm curious." Then she saw the gun, her green eyes widening. It was a .32 automatic. Alton checked the clip and it was loaded. He chambered a round and slipped the tool into the pocket of his windbreaker.

"Honk the horn," Alton instructed. "And let's get out of here."

Liz obliged. Upon hearing the signal, Spivey turned off his flashers and drove out of the motel parking lot, turning onto Sixty-seventh to return to I-35.

"Where's he going?"

"Back to the office, to await further instructions."

"Where are we going?" she asked without humor.

"Turn left," Alton said. The eastern sky was gray and darkening. Alton tossed the empty briefcase from the passenger window. And thought about Louisville and Monique. "Turn right," he said, studying the mirror.

"Do you think the car's safe?" Liz asked. In a few more moments, they'd need their headlights. "I mean, if that sleazeball would steal my earrings and take jewelry off a dead man . . ."

"It's safe." If it wasn't, his job was over, Alton thought. Liz could return to Chicago and play dress-up. Alton could hang the rail at Churchill Downs and box exactas in the Kentucky Oaks. He'd had the right filly in that race three years running. It was his favorite bet.

He had Liz turn into the A & W Rootbeer drive-in. "Circle behind and park in one of the stalls, facing the street. Leave it running."

They ordered soft drinks.

"Tell me about Muleford again," Alton said. "What were the details of his alibi?"

"Hans said he was there late last night, at Mrs. Muleford's. And Hans said when he showed up in the morning, Muleford was pulling out of the driveway."

"Not good enough," Alton said.

"Doesn't that depend on what Mrs. Muleford says?"

"He could have come and gone fifty times. Liz, somebody put you in that trunk. And somebody sure as hell put Jennings in there. I think it was Muleford. It had to be Muleford."

"Why?"

"He's the only one I can think of who wouldn't have killed you, that's why." Alton looked at her closely. She was tired. He studied the traffic on the four-lane. A dark sedan parked across the street at Pete La Cock's boat shop caught his eye. Two men sat in the front seat and they weren't doing a damn thing. They were cops, Alton thought.

"Feigen doesn't fool me for a minute. The man's cold, Liz. He's all business. If he'd killed Jennings, he'd certainly have killed you. Same thing with Jack Soo's crowd."

Maybe they weren't cops. The car was running.

"Besides I thought you and Feigen were in cahoots," Alton said, chiding her.

"What about this Spivey guy then?" Liz asked.

"He works the sidelines, Liz. He's a lackey."

"Maybe he's moving up. Maybe Spivey's your blind spot."

Then he felt it. He couldn't see their faces, but he could feel their eyes watching him, watching Liz.

"Crap," Alton said with disgust.

"What?"

"Let's get out of here. Now."

"Our drinks are coming . . ." Liz stared.

"Now!"

She put it in reverse. A young girl in an orange-and-brown uniform, holding a metal tray, watched her customers pull away. She seemed resigned to this sort of thing. Liz turned on the headlights as they slipped onto the four-lane, heading toward the Missouri side.

"Go slow," Alton said. He rolled down the window and adjusted the side-mounted mirror. The sedan was right behind them. They'd watched the drop, he thought. They were Spivey's men. Alton should have been driving.

CHAPTER SEVENTEEN

A gambler gets used to being wrong some of the time. It's a matter of statistics. And prison gives a criminal plenty of time to think over his mistakes. Alton chewed the inside of his lower lip, watching the trap close in around them.

At Roe Boulevard another car pulled into the slackening traffic. It moved from behind the first tail to the front of the van and maintained a constant speed. The cars were in radio contact.

Alton could have had Liz turn onto a side street and give it the gas through the residential section, but losing them didn't seem possible unless he was driving. They were locals and Liz was from out of town. Alton carefully considered his position and for the time being it seemed safe enough. As long as he had the car, they wouldn't hurt him. At least, they wouldn't kill him—yet.

At Mission Road a white limousine joined the trail. And at Rainbow Boulevard, Alton watched the fireball come on behind the front grill of the sedan directly behind them. It wasn't Spivey's men. Alton had been wrong about that.

"Change lanes and turn left at State Line."

"State Line?"

"The next light."

"Is he stopping us? I wasn't speeding."

"Apparently. And I guarantee you it's not a traffic cop. Go ahead and signal."

The car in front of them turned left at the light from the wrong lane, edging out the van. The fireball stayed on the van's bumper, while the stretch limo had to wait at the intersection when the left-turn arrow went off.

"Pull into that lot," Alton said dejectedly. "Is your door locked?"

Liz turned the van into the circle drive of the Pembroke Hill Day School.

"Stop here," Alton said grimly.

"Are you getting out?"

The option wasn't Alton's. He recognized the man outside his window as one of the two men who'd been escorted from his room at the Alameda that afternoon. The other one appeared at Liz's window. So much for a criminal trespass charge keeping a man in jail.

Alton heard the metal clicks of Liz's handcuffs, as the man at his side made an exaggerated cranking motion with one hand to have Alton roll the window down. He complied.

"The fireball's a nice touch," Alton said to the face that was all business and none of it official. "What does that setup cost anyway?" Liz was also rolling down her window.

"The key," the man on her side said.

She looked at Alton for permission. He nodded. She handed out the ignition key with her right hand. The man on Alton's side placed a blue-metal gun on the bottom edge of Alton's window. It's a bad feeling to have a gun pointed at your chest from less than a foot away. The man watched Alton's hands.

"If you're carrying heat, leave it behind. It's on you, hand it to me."

From the corner of his vision, Alton saw a similar weapon balanced on Liz's window. Alton had never liked the idea of shootouts. He'd have left Tombstone the day before that mess at the O.K. Corral.

"I have a gun in my jacket pocket," Alton informed his assigned lifeguard. The man opened the passenger door after unlocking it with his gun hand. The dome light came on. He wasn't a friendly-looking fellow. And he certainly wasn't a cop.

But the guy was comfortable with guns. He took Alton's from his windbreaker pocket, removed the clip and slipped it into his own pocket. With a quick little grin, he ejected the round in the chamber and let it bounce on the pavement. He tossed the gun onto the floorboard at Alton's feet. Alton hoped the gunman was too caught up in his work to notice what was under the seat.

"Both of you come with us," Alton's escort directed.

"Can't," Liz said, surprising Alton. She held up her left hand which was once again handcuffed to the steering wheel. "He lost the key," she added spitefully, as if rubbing it in. "We were on our way to find a . . ."

"Forget it," the man on Alton's side finally said, his gun in his jacket pocket along with his firing hand. That was a nice move on her part, Alton thought. Even if she was a crummy driver.

Alton climbed out of the van as his man took two steps backward. The other came around the front of the van to close the door for Alton, turning off the light. Their faces were shadows as the three of them, Alton in the middle, strolled to the limousine that had parked behind the secret sedan, peopled by another pair of friendly thugs. These were Jack Soo's fabled associates.

Another of the entourage stepped out of the rear of the white limousine, spilling yellow light on the pavement.

"Open his shirt," he ordered.

One of the escorts reached forward to do it, but Alton held up a hand. He unbuttoned his shirt and held it open, feeling a lot less super than Superman. The man from the limo only glanced at Alton's tattoo of a fighting cock on his chest, then motioned him into the luxury car, climbing in behind.

Alton was greeted by a man with three chins, large teeth and a thin gray mustache. He said his name was

John. His face was pink in the interior light and looked recently shaved. The limo smelled of expensive cologne and when the door was pulled closed the light didn't go out.

There were three of them, the bodyguard settling in on the seat next to John. Alton squatted uncomfortably on the jump seat, facing them.

"I don't have a lot of time," John said, his breath smelling strongly of onions. "Do you know who I am?"

"I have an idea," Alton said, thinking it bad luck to speak John's full name, as if reporters from the paper might show up to write it down. Then the FBI would call Alton downtown . . .

"I have an idea who you are, too, Rooster Franklin," he said slowly, as if secret meanings were contained in his words. "That's good enough to do business, don't you think so?"

Who was Alton to argue? John nodded to his bodyguard and Alton was handed an unsealed envelope. "Go ahead, read it," he was told and Alton did. Inside was a cashier's check for $15,000. It was made out to Alton Benjamin Franklin and countersigned by a bank clerk.

"You know what that is?"

Alton could guess, but he had no reply.

"It's the interest on two million dollars," John informed him. "You know how long it takes two million to make you fifteen grand?"

Alton shook his head.

"One month, my friend. That's one month's interest from a lousy savings account." He paused, letting it sink in.

Alton handed the check across the space separating him and the bodyguard.

"Keep it," John demanded. Alton placed the envelope inside his shirt and fumbled closed two buttons, covering his tattoo. "You have my phone number, Rooster. Did you lose it?"

"No, sir," Alton said.

"Then we have a deal, young man," John concluded, showing his teeth.

"No, sir."

The mobster didn't miss a beat. He motioned to his companion, who handed to Alton a bankbook and a pink card. The pink slip was a signature card. It was made out in Alton's name, along with an account number. He opened the bankbook and saw that $2 million had been deposited to open the account.

"This is the amount you and Mr. Soo agreed upon, is it not?"

Alton didn't respond.

"Sign it, Rooster," John ordered.

The bodyguard handed him a pen.

"I don't think I should," Alton tried to backpedal.

"You have no choice. You've done a good job and my company pays well for a job done right. I have no quarrel with you or your fee."

"Jennings wants the car back," Alton tried, testing John. If the mobster turned angry, if he knew that Alton was telling a lie, then it was Jack Soo's associates who'd killed Forrest Jennings. And it was John and his company who would kill Liz. Instead, John laughed. Without smiling.

"You blow up a man's house and he's nowhere around," he said. "What does that tell you, Rooster Franklin? What does that mean?"

"I don't know."

"He's out of town, Rooster. Take it from me, Jennings is not in the picture."

Enough said. Alton signed the card on his knee and returned it along with the bankbook and the pen to the bodyguard. If anyone had the proper line on this fiasco it was the pink-faced man sitting across the seat from Alton.

"Do you know James Spivey?" Alton had to ask.

John nodded, showing teeth.

"He hired me to steal the car," Alton said.

"Yes?"

"Do you know who for?"

"Yes of course. Harold Muleford is a friend of mine. We do business. He doesn't know what things are worth unless it's a truck. But, I tell you the truth, Rooster, he will not mind if I get the car. He will be happy for me. You won't have any problems with him."

Alton wished he could count on that.

"You see, this car is not for me, Rooster," John explained. "I want it for my country. I think the people should be able to see this car. Jack Kennedy was a better man than his brother."

Alton didn't want to get into a debate. And he sure as hell didn't want to end up arguing who'd killed Marilyn Monroe with one of the few people in America who probably knew for certain. The three of them thought about what John had said for a moment, then the mobster changed tracks.

"You like horses," John said. "Maybe someday I'll give you a hot tip."

John was flexing his clout. Alton knew exactly what he referred to. When he first began to play the horses, the idea that an occasional race was fixed bothered Alton tremendously. At this point in his gambling career, fixed races, like accidental deaths, were part of the stats.

"You call me when it's ready, Rooster," John directed. "When it's ready *tonight*. We come by and pick it up and we leave your paperwork behind. For this, you get fifteen grand for the rest of your life."

Alton nodded. All he wanted was to be let out of the limo.

"You go ahead and cash that check," John urged. "I don't make bad deals, Rooster. Do you understand me?"

What he understood was that John had no tolerance for anyone who might renege on a deal.

"Before you go, what's your girlfriend know about this?"

"Nothing," Alton lied. "She thinks I stole some jewelry."

"I don't believe you. But I understand. Me? I keep my women out of my business. It's the best way. Maybe you should dump this one. That's my advice. Send her off somewhere by herself and tell her you'll be there soon. There are a lot of girlfriends in this country for a man with two million dollars."

It was a lucky break. They'd confused Isabel Buddery with Monique. Of course John didn't believe him. Monique had been present in the hotel room when Jack Soo had made the original offer.

Alton was let out of the limousine. But John was finished.

"One more thing," the mobster called to him and Alton leaned back inside the light. "You don't deliver the car tonight, Rooster, and I've promised that check to whoever gets it back from you before the banks open tomorrow morning." He smiled for the first time. "It's part of a contract. Do you understand?"

Of course Alton understood. It wasn't as if John Ardella spoke a foreign language.

CHAPTER EIGHTEEN

Alton handed Liz the key and replaced the clip in Spivey's .32 automatic. There was no sense carrying a gun if it wasn't ready, Alton thought as he chambered a round and slipped it into his windbreaker pocket.

"Drive," Alton said.

"Where to?"

"Just drive."

The sedans had left the school parking lot, with the white limousine not far behind. Liz put the van into gear, then placed her head on the steering wheel as she was overcome with spasms of uncontrolled laughter. Alton thought at first she was weeping. Then, watching her, he couldn't help but grin.

"What is it?"

"Did you see . . ." she began, but was laughing again. Alton wished he could make her laugh like that. It was out of character for the aloof woman in white. "Did you see the look on his face?" Liz managed to ask after starting over three times.

Alton waited.

"When I . . . when I held up my handcuff?" There were tears on her face, she laughed so hard. Alton laughed with her. It was a regular riot.

Perhaps it was the tension. Or maybe they were going insane. The whole thing seemed awfully funny for a few moments. Alton unlocked both handcuffs, between his own outbursts of mad laughter.

Eventually they were back on the parkway. The headlights left too much of the night in darkness after the laughter died.

"What did they want?" Liz asked.

"To give me money. Everyone wants to give me money."

"What are you going to do with the car?" Liz asked outright.

"I was thinking of raffling it off for the Mayor's Christmas Fund." He cut through his own glib response by adding truthfully, "I really don't know, Liz."

Muleford said he didn't want the car. Alton considered the possibility that he hadn't been lying.

"What about the body?"

"What about it?" If Muleford didn't want the SS 100 X, why had he hired Alton to bid more than 13 million on the car?

"What are you going to do with it?"

"It's already done," Alton said, distracted. Alton had to face one fundamental fact. He'd been hired from the beginning to steal the car, not to bid on it. He knew that, but somehow kept forgetting it. The fact was Harold Muleford had hired Alton to steal the car, he repeated to himself.

"What do you mean, *It's already done?*"

"It's at the bottom of the Mighty Mo," Alton said. "The late Forrest Jennings is fish bait."

"Are you telling me the truth?"

"Nothing but," Alton said. "There was little to be gained by keeping it around. Except that the murder could have been pinned on me. Or you."

"So that's what your biker friend did for you?" Liz asked rhetorically. Alton realized his mistake the moment she said it. But at the time, getting rid of the corpse seemed the only logical thing to do. And the Missouri River was famous for its mud. It was as good a burial as any. Catfish weren't all that different from worms.

"You better turn around," Alton suggested. "Unless you want to spend the night at the Kansas City zoo."

"Speaking of which, why don't we get a room? I feel like we've been living in this van."

Alton felt like a target in a shooting gallery, moving back and forth in front of a gun. He didn't know whether sitting still was a much better idea, however. Between them, they already had three hotel rooms rented in Kansas City. What would another hurt? It would give Alton room to pace and he'd need to use the phone before the night was through.

They picked up supplies, including two sacks of burgers and fries from a nearby fast-food drive-through. Alton checked them into a room at a Best Western where Rainbow Boulevard turned into Seventh Street on the Kansas side. The motel was at the edge of Rosedale, a small community that had long ago been swallowed by the city. It was Alton's old neighborhood.

Liz took a shower. It was what she wanted to do. Alton stretched out, facedown on one of the beds, listening to the sound of running water. He tried not to think of her wet body under the warm spray. He closed his right eye, attempting to comfort it with darkness. The swelling had gone down.

Who was there left to ask? Feigen had said something in the lobby of the Alameda that now echoed in Alton's thoughts. *You should have talked to me.* Of course, Alton thought, Feigen was the only one at the auction, besides Muleford, who might have known the truth.

Alton rolled over on his back with a groan and picked up the telephone. Meza had had plenty of time to dispose of Forrest Jennings. Alton could count on that much having been done, which left him in the clear of being charged with murder. He pictured Liz with her eyes closed, the small bar of motel soap between her palm and belly. There was no way around the fact that whoever killed Jennings needed her dead.

He should have talked to Feigen. Alton dialed the local Associated Press stringer.

"Mark Revzin, please."

"Yeah, who's this?"

"Rooster," Alton said.

"No kidding. Look, Franklin, I'm on the machine. Nice talking to you."

"Wait!"

"Yeah?"

"I need some information."

"Fresh out."

"Dammit, Mark, will you give me a second?"

"You keeping me busy while somebody else is stealing my car?"

Revzin had every right to be angry. He and Alton had once been friends. To elude a rather sticky situation, Alton had once been forced to steal Revzin's car. The 1964 Corvette got the worst of it when introduced to a Kansas City elm at the end of a rainy street. Revzin didn't prefer charges, told the police he didn't have even the haziest idea who might have stolen his prized Stingray and never spoke to Alton again.

"I'm in a jam," Alton stressed. "I'm trying to keep a girl from getting killed."

"And I just thought you were calling to get the early spread on a basketball game," Revzin said sarcastically. "Jeez, Franklin, if I'd have known you were out rescuing damsels in distress . . ."

"Give me a minute, will you? This is serious."

"Do I get any details?" Revzin smelled a story.

"Forrest Jennings."

"Yeah?"

"You know him?"

"Of course," Revzin replied. "We got a whole computer disk of nothing but."

"First, tell me about this rumor," Alton requested. "You know, the women."

"Aw shit, Franklin. We can't use anything like that. You think we're the *National Enquirer* or something?"

"No," Alton said. "They pay better."

"That's no lie."

"Just fill me in on it, okay? The story's something different."

"He likes young girls and he likes to make videos. That's about it. Common knowledge but it's not for print."

"That's all?"

"Word is he and this guy, uh, Jay Barnett, distribute a few blue videos. Bondage-type stuff. Supposed to be shot in Jennings' basement. And the rich guy himself is said to, uh, have a starring role in each and every. But he wears a mask or something like that. Stage makeup, the works."

"He couldn't be identified," Alton commented.

"Not without a computerized voice analysis or something along those lines. In case you haven't heard, there's not a whole lot of talking in these things. Usually have some sort of elevator music laid over the sound track."

"Always the actor," Alton said. "It makes sense." The auction itself had been quite a performance, Alton realized. And not just by Muleford.

"Probably just a hobby for the old guy. Barnett more than likely is in on whatever money there is. It's my guess that Jennings just enjoys being in the movies. And getting his rocks off."

"You said bondage?"

"Whips and chains, you know. A few foreign objects."

"One more thing," Alton said, thinking. "You keep a social file on these rich guys, don't you?"

"We don't release that anymore. Used to be these clowns went to Cannes for the festival or attended some awards banquet in New York, they wanted everyone to know. Now, they put it on hold till they get back. Too

many burglaries are set up that way. *You* should understand that, Franklin."

"What about Jennings?"

"Are you kidding me? You're a known thief, pal. Besides, somebody already hit his place this morning.
They're passing it off as a natural-gas leak. Next thing you
know we'll be doing a story about the deterioration of
gas piping in Kansas City."

"Listen, Mark, you wouldn't mind a national byline,
would you? I got something you could put on the wire
tonight. Just give me Jennings' calendar for the past
month or so."

Revzin moaned. And he told him a few tidbits Alton
hadn't known.

Liz did not come out of the shower wearing only a towel,
wrecking Alton's fantasy. She'd pulled her clothes back
on. But her dark hair was still wet and she smelled
ninety-nine and forty-four one-hundredths percent
pure. He'd just dialed Spivey's number. It was that other
six-tenths of one percent of Liz he worried about.

"Working late?" Alton teased when Spivey answered
the phone.

"Okay, Franklin, you've been paid. I want the car."

"What about the body? Any ideas what I should do
with that? Maybe you want it back."

"What body? What are you talking about?" the attorney asked, playing dumb. Liz stopped towel drying her
hair to listen. She sank slowly onto a far corner of the
other bed, her back to Alton. He stared at her as he
continued to talk to Spivey.

Taking his turn in the bathroom, Alton removed his
shirt. He'd left his windbreaker in the other room, but
not his gun. The slim automatic was tucked inside his

jeans, behind his belt buckle. He'd been especially careful to make certain the safety was on. Alton didn't feel half as cocky as the rooster on his chest. He was tired now and distracted by a vague and unrequited lust.

Her white nylon panties hung on the shower-curtain rod, drying quickly even in the moist air of the bathroom. He hung the cool, diaphanous material over the hook on the back of the door and was overtaken with crazy thoughts about the zipper of Isabel Buddery's black slacks.

Alton turned on the shower. He let it run awhile. Then, for added effect, he began to croon a Beatles lyric, standing on the bathroom mat, waiting. She could walk out if she wanted to, if she were the least bit quiet about it.

With a suddenness he hadn't quite intended and feeling a lot like Eliot Ness, Alton threw open the bathroom door and rushed into the motel room. She'd fallen for it.

"Calling Mom?" Alton asked.

Liz quietly put down the phone, unable to hide the fear in her startled, green eyes. They gave her away, those eyes. Alton looked at her, blinking, bringing his blind spot into sharp focus. Her eyes were on his gun.

"Well, you've had your shower, Liz," he said, trying not to dislike her. "Isn't it time you come clean?"

Alton honed in on her, seeing things that he'd seen before but that he'd somehow missed. She looked good for a woman who was trapped, though her lower lip trembled slightly.

"Who do you work for?"

Liz recoiled.

"Who were you calling?" He strode purposefully toward her. Liz leaned back on the bed where she was sitting, planting a splayed hand on the mattress. Clearly, she was thinking through the different things she could say, the stories she could fabricate.

"Who?"

Alton stood between the beds. Liz looked fitfully cornered, ready for flight. Alton pictured her clambering over the bed, like a hamster let out of its cage, scurrying blindly along the walls toward the door. He didn't want to point the gun. Not at Liz. Alton didn't want to see her shrink.

"You weren't hired by Harold Muleford," Alton began for her. "That much is clear to me. Harold didn't need you there. The only person he needed there was me. He wasn't bidding on the car, Liz. Now, who were you calling?"

CHAPTER NINETEEN

"He wasn't there," she said weakly. "No one answered and I'm telling the truth."

"Who?" Alton repeated.

"Are you going to hit me?"

"Feigen?"

"No."

"Who then? John Ardella, Jack Soo?"

She shook her head.

"Or was it Mr. Nobody, what's his name, David Cross?"

She shook her head again, looking down at her feet. The hair around her face had begun to dry. It curled in on her eye from one side. Liz brushed it away, tugging it behind her ear with a shaky hand. She looked like a little girl to Alton when she did that.

"I thought you were taking a shower," Liz blurted out, as if he had cheated. Like all women, Liz lived and judged people by a secret set of moral rules. A man never knew what they were until he'd broken one. Faking a shower to get the drop on a phone call obviously breached Isabel Buddery's code of ethical behavior. Alton was a man who couldn't be trusted.

"You want the car, Liz. Let's start with that. You want the car for somebody else. There's no reason to make things up now. Who were you calling?"

"Nicholas McCorkle."

"Okay, I'll believe that. Is he your boss in Chicago?"

"Here."

"But you're still from Chicago, aren't you?"

"Yes." She still wouldn't look at him.

"And you met Muleford there?"

"Yes."

"But he didn't hire you?"

"That's correct."

"How about Jennings? Had you met him before?"

"No," she answered, back to her one-word responses that Alton found far more believable than any previous elaborations. Yet, her responses had the unmistakable ring of courtroom testimony. Then it came to him.

"You're a cop," he accused, knowing he was right.

"Was a cop," Liz corrected him.

"What's the new career then, Liz? Private detective?"

"Federal investigator," she said, as if being charged with being a private detective was synonymous with having a contagious and disfiguring disease named after you.

"How is J. Edgar Hoover these days, still dead?"

Alton plopped down on the edge of the opposite bed, his knees beside hers in the alley between the two beds. Liz glanced at him, then glanced quickly away. She had the best face he'd ever seen on a federal investigator.

"Not the FBI," she said. "I work for the Department of Agriculture."

Alton rolled his eyes. "You've got to be kidding."

"No, Frankie, I'm not." Alton could count on one hand and still keep his thumb tucked in his belt loop the number of times Liz had called him by his name. "Each federal department has an investigative branch."

"So what do you do, check for crooked corn rows? Arrest people for growing melons with the stripes running the wrong way?"

"Food stamps. It's an incredibly large black market. It ties in with a lot of other things."

"So you bust some welfare case because he'd rather have fifty bucks cash to buy cigarettes and beer with than have a hundred dollars in food stamps?"

"Or Tampax or toilet paper. Food stamps aren't valid for a lot of necessities. But we go after the buyers. Not the sellers. There are traders who turn a million dollars on underground food stamps a month. There are bookies downtown who take food stamps at half value to settle an account. And you know who the bookies work for. There are other things, too."

Alton lifted his eyebrows. He supposed there was a million dollars to be made from stolen toothpicks if you set it up right.

"Forged USDA approval seals for one thing. And there's the commodity exchange. That falls under our domain."

"Pork bellies," Alton said absently. "But what's the USDA want with the SS 100 X?"

"Oh that," Liz said without a pause, "I'm on loan to the Department of the Treasury on this one. I didn't have to wear a wire, so I thought why not?"

"The Secret Service of course. They lost the car in the first place and now they want it back."

"They want it off the market," Liz explained. "The car isn't supposed to exist. It goes public and there'd be no end to the embarrassment. Frankie, there are still people who think the assassination was a conspiracy."

Alton took his thumb out of his belt loop. She'd called him by his name twice in the past ten minutes. He liked the sound of it.

"If this car surfaces," she went on, "all the kooks with all the kooky theories will come out of the woodwork and the Secret Service's reputation will be shot."

"So to speak," Alton said grimly.

"You know, of all the studies done on the assassination, there's one thing on which everyone agrees."

"The Secret Service blew it," Alton said.

Liz nodded. "Worse than that. Technically, they were responsible for the President's safety. So, technically they were at fault. But a madman in an upstairs window can shoot just about anyone he wants."

"They shouldn't have gone to Dallas in the first place."

"That's hindsight. Too easy. It's like saying Lincoln shouldn't have gone to the theater that night."

Alton knew a lot about hindsight. It was always quite clear to him which horse should have been wagered on after the race was done.

"I knew a guy who got sent up on a convenience store robbery," Alton told her. "It was January and he walks in and strong-arms the clerk. Gets about two hundred bucks and runs off into the night. The police showed up, followed the tracks in the snow seventeen blocks to this guy's apartment. They arrested him with the money spread out on the kitchen table. Four years later and he still blamed the weather for his getting caught."

"The agent driving the SS 100 X could have saved the President's life is what I'm talking about," Liz said. "After the first shot, nobody was dead. If the driver had swerved at that instant, if he'd sped up or stamped on the brakes, the second and third shots would have missed. But he didn't know the President was being shot. The agents in the car behind him did. They got on the radio to tell him, but it was too late.

"We don't know what he could have seen in the rear-view mirror, but he knew something was happening. He just couldn't see *what* was happening until it was over."

"Blind spot," Alton said. "But it's not like he was at fault."

"Nobody was at fault," Liz insisted. "But you can imagine how they felt. The driver, the other agents. They worked with him every day. They knew when he'd nicked his neck shaving and when he hadn't gotten a good night's sleep. They loved this man, Frankie. More than all those weeping ladies on television the next day."

Alton thought it over. "I remember where I was that day. I guess everyone does. They announced it over the loudspeakers at school. Miss Briscoe, our teacher, broke down crying. That's what scared us, her crying like that. They let us out early that day and we all went home and watched it on television."

They were silent for a moment.

"When were you born anyway?" Alton asked.

"December, 1963."

"Figures." He'd thought she was older.

"But I was there, too. I was told about it all my life. My mother went into false labor when Kennedy was shot. My middle name is Kennedy. I grew up with his picture on the wall. I thought John-John was my older brother."

"In England?"

"Fort Leavenworth," she said. "My father was RAF. He was stationed there, taught special-training schools for the U.S. Army. He was a language specialist. It's where he met my mother."

"Retired?"

"Dead. So's Mom."

"I'm sorry," Alton said automatically.

"Natural causes," Liz replied blankly. "A car wreck. Their six minutes were up."

Alton stood up, stretching his legs. They'd follow him now, wherever he went. He pushed past Liz and picked up the telephone. After speaking loudly to a woman who had trouble hearing over the background music, Alton got Meza on the line.

"It's time to move the car," Alton said. He looked at Liz. If someone had answered her phone call, she could have told them where the SS 100 X was before he burst out of the bathroom like gangbusters.

"You're going to have to tow it. I've got the key and I don't want the wires ripped."

Liz vigorously wiggled her right earlobe, between thumb and forefinger, at Alton. It took him a moment to understand what she wanted, then he waved her off to deal with Meza's protests.

"Trust me," Alton said into the phone. "You don't want me to come around. I'm hot."

Meza relented. Alton gave him the specific route he was to follow. Liz pouted dramatically at Alton, her fists on her hips.

"What about the jewelry?" Alton said.

"That's my business, brother," Meza said, offended. "It's out of here."

"The girl," Alton tried to explain. "She lost her earrings and wants to know if you picked them up?"

Meza cursed. Alton shook his head to let Liz know he'd received a negative response. Then he went over the route again before hanging up.

"I know you think I'm being stupid," Liz said. "But they're very expensive. The department borrowed them for me to wear to the auction. Thirty thousand, wholesale. I could lose my job."

"You could always be a stewardess," he said.

"Screw you."

Alton wished. "It's a write-off," he said. "You must have lost them at Jennings' place, after you were unconscious. I don't think it's a good idea to go back for them."

"McCorkle's going to kill me," she sighed dejectedly.

"Right now, he's going to have to stand in line behind Jennings' murderer."

Alton phoned the number Jack Soo had given him. As soon as Alton said who he was, he was patched in to John Ardella. The connection was poor and Alton suspected Ardella was riding around in his white limo. He told John much the same thing he'd told Spivey earlier on the phone.

Then he called the Westin Crown Center and asked for Rick Feigen. No one answered the phone in the CIA operative's hotel room. Alton called back and, as a lark, asked for Isabel Buddery. She was registered there. And, thankfully, no one answered the phone in her room either.

"Would Feigen have me followed?" Alton asked Liz.

"You want to know the truth?"

"It's a refreshing change I could get used to."

"They've been following you all along," she said. "He put an electronic beeper on your van when you brought me to your hotel this morning. They're waiting for you to lead them to the car."

"Are you sure?"

"I checked. It's inside the rear bumper of your van. They've kept back far enough, you haven't seen them."

"And the CIA came in on this one alone?"

"More or less. They don't mind the Treasury Department getting the car back. But they'd blow up the SS 100 X before they let it out of the country. They're afraid of a hostage situation."

"A car-napping?"

"It could happen. Feigen contacted me just before the auction. He explained everything. I was supposed to have the best chance of winning the bid."

"Were you really going to buy the car?"

"Yes," Liz said.

"That's where all those tax dollars go!" Alton exclaimed.

Liz shook her head. "It was a small price to pay, Frankie. You've got to understand how special the SS 100 X is. It's easily the most valuable car in existence."

"Did you get in touch with Feigen today?"

"No."

"McCorkle then?"

"No," she said, pulling her loose hair behind her ear again. Alton didn't know why, but he believed her. He looked at his watch. There was still plenty of time. He picked up the phone and called a cab. Alton had everything but the murder figured out. He'd given himself to midnight to work on that puzzle.

CHAPTER TWENTY

Alton and Liz darted out a side door off a connecting hall of the Best Western and climbed into the backseat of the waiting cab. His phone calls hadn't managed to call off the heat. They'd been spotted leaving and picked up a tail on Rainbow Boulevard. It looked like one of Ardella's sedans.

Alton gave the cabby detailed directions. They turned east on Forty-third Street, turned south then on Roanoke, then east again on Forty-seventh, slipping in the back door of the Country Club Plaza. Alton had the driver let them out on the top level of a Plaza parking garage. The sedan pulled smoothly into one of the marked-off slots and killed the headlights.

The driver of the sedan, however, had left his foot on the brake pedal, the red glow of his rear brake lights giving him away. It was a mistake Alton had long ago learned not to make. Alton was a better car thief than any soldier in the Kansas City mob.

Using the enclosed overhead walkway, Alton led Isabel Buddery into Seville Square, along a subtle maze of canyon-like corridors and stairwells done up in plaster statuary. One man from the car followed them.

"Act casual," Alton said, easing an arm around Liz's waist. "We're going to a movie."

The theater was in the lower level, across from one of those one-hour-service photo shops. Alton and Liz stood in line, watching through the nearby window somebody's snapshots of what must have been a birthday party come rolling out of the printer.

"Are we being followed?" Liz wanted to know.

"It's the price you pay for being popular," Alton whispered in her ear.

Of the four movies showing, Alton bought tickets to the one that hadn't already started. It was a Dirty Harry feature. Just the thing to settle your stomach when you were on the run from the mob, the CIA, Sargent Security, Inc. and an unknown murderer. To make it look real, Alton bought a bucket of buttered popcorn and two large diet sodas.

Alton remembered to close one eye before walking into the darkened theater. He caught a peep of their tail, who hung around outside the lobby, reading the marquees. He was buying it, Alton thought.

On a weekend the movie would have sold out. Alton and Liz had no trouble finding two seats near the back. They munched popcorn while the previews rolled. Alton was giving it ten minutes. Any longer than that and their tail might figure things out.

He set aside the popcorn and held her hand. Alton was as surprised as when he'd been fourteen and tried it for the first time that she let him. If he were young again, Alton would ask girls to the movies every night.

"I kissed you," he said quietly under the blaring sound track. "Did you know that?"

"What?" Liz asked, leaning close to him, her green eyes riveted on the screen. "I didn't hear you."

"They'll wait an hour and a half," he said. Their tail should have bought a ticket. Alton figured the guy had already seen the show. Alton wondered if the guy back in the parking lot had taken his foot off the brakes yet.

"Whenever you're ready," Liz told him, catching on to the plan. She continued watching the movie with rapt intensity and curled her fingers tightly over the back of Alton's hand.

In Japan, porcelain dolls are traditionally sold without the eyes painted on. When you were given the doll as a present, you made a wish and painted on one eye. When the wish came true, you painted on the other one. As Liz warmly squeezed his hand, Alton painted the first eye, a wide green circle inside two black lines.

"Let's go," he finally said. They sat down their drinks on the floor and Alton regretted having to let go of her hand. They strode down the aisle, ducked quickly across the flickering screen and slipped out a curtained doorway under a red EXIT sign.

The hallway led to a short flight of stairs up to the side street away from the parking garage. Alton opened the door and stepped into the night air. There was traffic everywhere. Taking Liz's hand, he guided her across the street, circling behind one of the numerous horse-drawn carriages on the Plaza at night. He'd never ridden in one and had never wanted to. Until tonight.

They circled two more blocks in the crowd, that included more than the average number of women in furs. It wasn't a cold night, but furs were one of the popular means of conveyance between the bars and the restaurants on the Country Club Plaza at night. Alton and Liz came across a McDonald's that, in keeping with the Plaza's scheme of things, had a bronze statue out front of a boy on a rock. He held a book in one hand and a metal hamburger in the other.

"A few thousand years and the archaeologists will have fun with that one," Alton said.

At the end of the street they caught a cab. Again Alton's directions were specific.

"What's missing," he told Liz in the backseat, "is Barnett. Where was Barnett in all this? He lived in the house. He should have been there when Jennings was shot. He should have been there when you were stuffed into the trunk."

"Maybe he did it," Liz said.

"I don't think so. He and Jennings had too much going on. If he were going to sell out, he would have done it long ago. Muleford would have offered him plenty of opportunities."

"Maybe he was Muleford's plant, working both ends all along."

That was an idea worth considering. It would explain why Muleford was there to handle the police and the press after the bomb went off and Alton had driven the car away.

"Are we going back?" Liz asked when Alton told the driver to turn north onto Rainbow Boulevard.

Alton shook his head. There was a large apartment complex at the bottom of a steep rise along the west side of Rainbow as it curved toward the Best Western and Southwest Boulevard. Meza surely had moved the car by now.

It was dark behind the last apartment building. A cat scampered out of one of the trash dumpsters and screeched as they approached the wooden fence. A small, startled cry escaped her lips, and Alton put his arm around Liz.

"You any good at climbing fences?" he asked. It was a rhetorical question. The apartment complex was enclosed by what Alton called a Popsicle fence, vertical slats with rounded tops nailed to three cross two-by-fours between four-by-four posts eight feet apart. They always put the two-by-fours on the inside, so people would have trouble getting in.

Climbing out was as easy as climbing three large steps and dropping six feet on the other side. Alton went first. As he hit the ground, it occurred to him this would be the perfect time for Liz to make a run for it if that's what she had in mind.

"Come on," he called anxiously, ready to help her down. Alton was relieved to see her hands, then dark hair appear at the top of the fence. She brought a knee up and over. Alton reached to lend his support, one hand propping up her buttocks. He'd seen cheerleaders held like this on televised basketball games and had always wanted it to be his hand.

Liz let go of the fence, turning into his arms. Alton let gravity slide her gently to the ground, inside his embrace, her belly, then her breasts against his chest. It was as good as having your picture on a Topps baseball card, having won a Golden Glove award for the catch of the decade.

"Are we dancing or what?" Liz asked, slightly embarrassed when Alton didn't release her right away. He could feel her breath on his cheek. Dancing wasn't the sport Alton had in mind.

They'd come down in the parking lot of the Rosedale State Bank. Cars slid by on the Rainbow curve, their headlights igniting the street, shoving shadows into the parking lot, wedging the night in around Alton and Liz at the bottom of the hill. He led her behind the bank to an unmarked and unlighted service road that led up the side of the hill.

In the distance, a dog barked. He held her hand as they climbed toward the Rosedale Arch. Alton paused on the narrow road between thickets of hillside scrub trees and turned to look toward Kansas City proper. You could see the lighted dome of the downtown Power and Light building from here. It changed colors all through the night. Right now it was green and Alton accepted that as a favorable sign.

But he could also see the Best Western at the end of Rainbow. Every car in the parking lot looked to be filled to the brim with bad guys, with people who wanted either Liz or Alton, or both of them, dead. At the top of the hill, the road opened onto a pitted and cracked parking lot.

"What's this?" Liz asked, staring at the three-story brick building.

"Rosedale High," Alton said. "At least, it used to be. Now it's mostly a warehouse. Maybe there's a community day-care center in the basement. They don't even use the place to vote in any longer."

Alton pointed out the Rosedale Arch at the far end of the athletic field. It was a model of the *Arc de Triomphe,* a local memorial to area residents who'd fought in World War I. At night, twin spotlights illuminated the arch and you could see it from just about everywhere in the neighborhood. If you knew to look up. Most people who drove Rainbow Boulevard didn't know it was there.

"It's huge," Liz said, staring at the arch.

"It looks bigger from up here," Alton admitted.

The chain-link gate to the athletic field had broken down years ago. Through the wet, overgrown grass and weeds of the field, Alton and Liz had walked ten yards beyond the felled and rusted goalposts before she saw it.

Liz stopped walking. Alton stood beside her in the dark field, feeling the breeze. A small airplane crossed over them, its wing-lights blinking as it descended. Propeller planes always sounded to Alton as if they were about to crash when they came in low for a landing at the downtown airport. Every few years, one of them ended up in the river.

Liz released his hand. The SS 100 X, its black top up, was parked under the Rosedale Arch, bathed in the indirect light of the memorial's spotlights. Liz wanted to ask if they were going to drive it. As if stung, Liz hurried away from him, toward the car, toward touchdown. She broke into a run.

The bleachers were sagged and empty. That was Alton's only regret. It was as if the game had been won and they were the heroes of their sport. But Alton knew, as he reached inside his windbreaker to ease the bite of the .32 automatic against his skin, that the game had really only just begun. Still, they should have sold tickets to this one.

CHAPTER TWENTY-ONE

Meza had left a six-pack of beer on the front seat of the SS 100 X. This meant their deal was completed. He'd come through for Alton and been well paid for a day's work.

Alton unlocked the driver's door and pocketed the key. He'd brought along everything else he would need. Holding open the door for Liz, he watched her climb in around the steering wheel. Alton was right behind her.

Meza had left the car parked with its front flags pointed toward the city. There was a lot to see from this end of the hill. Below them was a cut-through road from Rainbow to Southwest Boulevard. Across the road from them was the triangle of buildings, including their Best Western, a Shoney's and a string of new shops that fronted Rainbow. From behind the wheel, Alton watched the traffic lights change at the intersection of the two boulevards.

Beyond the intersection were the railroad tracks and the Bunge grain elevators. On a larger hill, the city landscape stood like a mirage. The dome of the Power and Light building remained green. You watched the handful of Kansas City skyscrapers long enough at night and the buildings appeared to move on you, subtly shifting positions. Alton pictured the tall buildings getting up and walking across the Missouri River to start a new city somewhere beyond the influence of people like John Ardella.

Liz said nothing. Alton opened a can of beer and

handed it to her. He opened one for himself. It was warm and foamy. It was too early to propose a toast.

There was time to kill. Alton felt like a kid with his father's car parked at some local lover's lane. Just as when he'd been fifteen, he could think of nothing to say. Just as it had been when he was fifteen, the night was spooky when you were sitting still. It was the perfect time for ghost stories and one in particular closed in around the two of them.

Alton was afraid to look into the passenger compartment of the limousine. The upholstery of the backseat had once been bathed in blood. Even on black-and-white television, you could see the crimson stain on Jackie's clothes. The events of that day didn't fit into a proper reality. The assassination was too huge, too overwhelming. It didn't fit into any sequence of events.

There was a long, gray crack in the asphalt of a Dallas street where a nation's innocence had fallen in.

"Are we going to say goodbye?" Liz asked from her corner of the darkness inside the 1961 Lincoln Continental.

Alton thought about saying goodbye. The murder was becoming clear to him. The spotlights on the Rosedale Arch reflected dully inside the SS 100 X, encircling Liz's features in a halo. The edges of her profile, her shoulders, her arms and her hair, glowed. A reflection from the can of beer dinted the darkness as she brought it to her mouth.

There's something about the proximity of death that makes people want to touch. Alton slipped his gun under the driver's seat. There were bombs going off. The trees were full of assassins. He wanted to make love to her. Alton reached for Liz to make his wish come true. As if he knew she would, Liz welcomed him.

It was a tight, desperate act. Liz clung to him with her green eyes open and dug her fingers into his back. She held on so tightly that she rose with him when Alton lifted from the waist. Agent Buddery buried her teeth in his shoulder to keep from crying out. It wasn't the kind of sex they make romantic movies about.

And when they were done, Alton painted the other emerald eye on his porcelain doll. He could now see in the dark. She was smiling at something. He would like to have kissed her lightly on the cheek, but the bombs were still going off. Rifles were pointed right at them.

"What are you smiling about?" he asked.

"Don't go getting a big head," Liz warned him. "Another six minutes went by and I'm still alive. That's all."

"That's worth something." *Alive* was a nice word for the way he felt.

Alton opened the driver's door and stood next to the dark blue limousine to get dressed. Liz found her sweater and pulled it on where she sat. Then Isabel Buddery attempted to fix her hair by running her hands through it.

"Here," he said, leaning in, handing her something cool to the touch. It was the pair of panties she'd left in their room to dry, the pair of white panties she'd been wearing when he'd lifted her from the trunk of the SS 100 X and had kissed her to bring her back to life.

He closed the door and walked to the edge of the hill, stepping on the chain-link fence that on this end of the field was entirely down, a tricky part of the rusty grass. Alton relieved himself beyond the glow of the Rosedale Arch. On the cut-through road at the bottom of the hill, Ardella's white limousine waited. He was early.

When he returned to the car, Alton found Liz dressed, hunched forward behind the steering wheel of the SS 100 X. She turned a key in the ignition switch over and over again. Alton tapped on the window glass.

"Won't work," he told her.

Eventually she gave up, unlocked the door from the inside and let him open it.

"Can't blame a person for trying," Liz said. She slid across the seat and Alton got back in behind the wheel.

"Where'd you get the key?"

"They had it made for me."

"No," Alton said, closing the door. "I mean *where* were you carrying it? When I found you this morning you weren't wearing anything but your . . ."

"It wasn't under my tongue," Liz said, cutting him off. Alton began to have more respect for the Department of Agriculture. That's what she'd bought that purse for, Alton recalled.

"This morning," he began, "when I found you in the trunk, I thought at first you were dead. And when I couldn't wake you up, I kissed you. It was as if I thought you were Sleeping Beauty and I was a prince."

"Don't be so hard on yourself. Maybe you are a prince, Frankie."

"But you're no Sleeping Beauty," he said quietly. "I've figured it all out."

"Are you going to give them the car?"

"People are such garbage bags," Alton said, ignoring her question.

"Up yours," Liz said with sudden venom. Women don't enjoy being insulted after sex.

"Not you, Liz. I mean all of us. We accept all this garbage, anything anybody wants to put into us, all that crap we read in the papers. We just take it in until we're crammed full of it. You never saw Forrest Jennings before the auction, did you?"

"No," she said.

"You never saw a picture of him either?"

"I guess not. What are you getting at?"

"Neither did I," Alton said. "I didn't know the man from a horse's ass. But we all assumed it was Jennings that night because it was his auction. It was his house. It was his car."

"It was never *his* car. Not really."

"That's not the point," Alton went on. "You, me, Jack Soo, David Cross . . . we'd never met the man. Don't you see? That's what Rick Feigen was trying to tell me. He's the only one in the whole group who'd done his homework on Jennings. The auction was a sham. Jennings wasn't even there."

"I don't see how . . ."

"It was Barnett," Alton continued. "Jennings has been out of the country for more than two weeks now. It's a fact, Liz. An indisputable fact."

Liz said nothing and Alton didn't blame her. She'd made a dreadful mistake.

"Muleford set up the whole thing. He wanted the car stolen. He wanted one of us to steal it, so he set it up. He never wanted the car itself. All he wanted was for it to be gone when Jennings came back. He was just getting one up on his arch rival.

"And who better to play Jennings than his right-hand man? I should have known something was up when that faker handed me a glass with more ice in it than scotch," Alton said.

"One of Muleford's stooges played Barnett. He wasn't very good at it. But Barnett himself did an excellent job of playing Forrest Jennings, especially when Muleford broke in with that duel of his. In the end, he played him too well. Barnett's little acting job cost him his life."

Alton waited for Liz to say something. Another car pulled up on the street below.

"You killed the wrong man, Liz," he said after a moment of harsh silence. "Apparently your jewelry wasn't the only thing you were wearing to bed."

Alton didn't watch her reaction. He didn't want to see it. He leaned forward and groped for the loaded .32 automatic he'd placed under the edge of the driver's side of the front seat. It was missing.

Alton's stomach knotted. He took a deep breath and for the hell of it found the switch that turned on the tiny spotlights that illuminated the flags mounted on the front fenders of the SS 100 X. He flipped the switch. The flags looked good lit up, even in the dead breeze.

"That's not all there is to it," Liz said. "You don't know what happened. You don't know how I felt."

Maybe, he thought.

"He brought a drink to my room and asked me to put my earrings on. I played along. I didn't know what else to do. He'd fixed up this room for me to stay in. I'd already seen the car. I was supposed to get it in the morning. He told me there was a way to get it out of the house."

"You knew what the man you thought was Jennings was going to do. You knew about his sexual tastes. The Secret Service had to have told you about all that."

"That's why they chose me," she said weakly. "I figured I was in for it. But when I sipped that drink, everything changed so suddenly. It was like gunshots going off. I knew instantly that I'd been drugged. It worked so damn fast, Frankie."

Liz was crying.

"It's okay," Alton said softly. "It's okay, Liz."

"No it's not," she blurted out. "Dammit, it's not. I thought he'd killed me. My purse was right there. He came forward, grinning like an ape. Everything was spinning . . . I couldn't let him . . ."

Listening to her voice break, Alton stared at the flags through the windshield. They looked like complicated stars plastered onto the night. They looked to be listening, watching. When he'd first met Liz, she'd seemed so sophisticated. She seemed older. The mysterious woman in white turned out to be about the same age as Monique. He heard the voice of a little girl as she went on with her story, pleading to be believed.

"I couldn't let him get away with killing me. I was so alone, Frankie. I was so scared. I thought I was dying."

"What did you do with your gun?"

"I shoved it between the mattresses. He fell across the

bed. I got up somehow. I remember making it to the bedroom door, then I collapsed. The next thing I recall was when you woke me up and you and that biker lifted his body out of the trunk."

"The gun's probably still there," Alton said.

"It doesn't matter," she said. Liz stopped crying and struggled to breathe in slow, regular intakes of air. "How did you know?"

"You never once accused me of having killed Jennings," Alton told her. He reached for her hand, but she took it away. "I was the most logical person to have killed him from your point of view. Unless of course you already knew who killed him.

"Then you kept backing off Muleford every time I was so certain he'd done it. Jack Soo wouldn't have murdered him without killing you. Same thing with Feigen, even though he knew it was Jay Barnett. Hell, Liz, nobody would have killed only one of you . . . unless the murderer *was* one of you."

Alton kept talking to give Liz a chance to collect herself.

"Spivey was working with Muleford all along," he said. "When Muleford's stooge heard the shots and found the two of you in the room, it started everything in motion. Muleford got his butt over there and set up his alibi with his ex-wife. He thought the way to handle it was to put both of you in the trunk. He knew I was supposed to steal the car.

"Then when I did he had to worry about somebody pinning the murder on him when the car didn't surface. He'd thought about that too late. He covered up the theft and then I came waltzing into his office. He's probably still shitting frogs, wondering what I'm up to.

"Hell, Muleford didn't even know for sure who'd killed his star actor. From what I gathered talking to Spivey, they thought it was me. That I hid in the closet and sneaked out the back door. They were setting me up when they put the bodies in the car, Liz. At least, that's what they thought."

"I'm sorry," Liz said. Alton was sorry, too, aware that Isabel Buddery referred now to what she was going to do, not to what she'd already done.

"There's no body, Liz; there's no murder," he said quickly. "You're clean."

"You can't let them have the car," she said firmly.

"What will the Secret Service do with it, Liz?"

"Chop it up into little pieces, I suppose." She sounded as if she regretted that.

"What would they do with it if people found out the SS 100 X still exists?"

"It's been covered, Frankie. They'll donate it to the Smithsonian. But it will come from them. That's important. It will come from the government to the people. It won't end up as some gaudy murder sideshow in one of the mob's Las Vegas casinos."

"I don't like being beat out by someone on salary," Alton said.

"I have your gun."

"I know. You won't need it."

They managed to get the hood open and Alton replaced the Lincoln's rotor cable he'd brought along with him. Liz walked with him to the edge of the hill. He filled her in on what was happening. A tractor-trailer rig pulled onto the side street with a guttural roar, its running lights looking like a crown along the top of the cab. A large jackrabbit was painted in mid-leap on the side of the trailer.

"Spivey must have decided he wants the car for himself," Alton said. "Or maybe Muleford's willing to find it a home, after all."

He pointed out the white limo to Liz. She recognized it.

"Ardella should be leaving soon," Alton said, checking his watch. The media was late to everything. He turned

back to look at the SS 100 X in the light of the Rosedale
Arch. Then looking up, Alton could see the stars. He had
read Shakespeare in prison. Will had written something
about death and stars.

> . . . When he shall die,
> Take him and cut him out in little stars,
> And he will make the face of heaven so fine
> That all the world will be in love with night
> And pay no worship to the garish sun.

"Who's that?" Liz asked. A blue van turned onto the
street at the foot of the hill. One of the local television
crews finally made it. Revzin had held up his end of the
bargain. Alton placed his key to the SS 100 X in her hand.

"Circle left around the back of the field," he instructed. "You'll come out on the parking lot. You get
down the hill the same way we walked up."

Liz closed her fingers around the key. She lifted on her
toes, facing him, and kissed Alton quickly on the cheek.
"You're a prince, Frankie," she said. He didn't believe it.
She left him there.

Halfway down the hill, she turned on the headlights to
alert the camera crew. Today, stars were born and died
on the flickering face of television. It was well after midnight when Alton made it down the hill.

The cut-through street was clear of parked traffic except for a red sports car. A small man was smoking a
cigarette, leaning against the trunk of the vehicle.

"Over here!" Alton called as he approached on foot,
four beers dangling from the plastic strap looped around
a finger of his left hand. The man waited until Alton
handed him a warm beer before speaking.

"Ready for that exclusive interview?" Mark Revzin
asked.

"I don't feel like talking," Alton said. "Give me a lift to
my van, will you?"

"I don't think so." The Associated Press reporter gave Alton a long, hard look. "I think I'd rather run over you in the street."

"Your time would be better spent driving to the airport. I'd be looking for a government cargo plane, if I were you. A C-130 perhaps."

Alton watched the taillights of the sports car turn the corner, and walked back to Rainbow, drinking a beer. In the Best Western parking lot, he removed the electronic beeper from his rear bumper and stuck it under the bumper of the car parked in the next slot.

He bought a postage stamp and a package of envelopes at an all-night truck stop on I-70 east of Kansas City. Alton wrote *No thank you* where you were supposed to endorse the cashier's check and sealed it inside the envelope he'd addressed to a Kansas City car dealership that John Ardella owned.

He was between St. Louis and Louisville when the sun came up. James Spivey would have some long-distance explaining to do. He should have known better than to hire a crook, Alton thought. Forrest Jennings was bound to miss Jay Barnett when he returned to town. He'd probably miss the SS 100 X, too. He could always visit it on one of his art-buying trips to the capital.

But Alton Benjamin Franklin couldn't worry about all that. He was in a hurry to check out the past performances of horses running at Churchill Downs. And there was a dark-eyed cocktail waitress somewhere in town to whom he wanted to give a pair of diamond-and-emerald earrings. He'd keep the President's driver's license for himself for a while. It was the sort of thing a patriotic prince with one sore eye was inclined to do.

About the Author

Author of the critically acclaimed *Hot Wire,* Randy Russell remains at large in midtown Kansas City, where he lives with his wife, Janet Barnett, and their indoor Great Dane, Desdemona. *Blind Spot* is his Crime Club debut.